GETTING SCOT AND BOTHERED

CAROLINE LEE

ABOUT THIS BOOK

Rocque Oliphant has simple wants: a fine sword at his hip, a good meal in his belly, and a lusty wench by his side. His position as the Oliphant Commander, leader of men, ensures the first, and his long-term affair with Merewyn, the clan healer, ensures the second and third. She brings him joy—and pleasure—in ways he once only dreamed of!

Aye, things are going well in his life...at least they were, right up until his father—the laird—demanded he marry and start producing grandsons. If Rocque wants to beat his brothers at a chance for the lairdship, he needs to find a willing woman to bear his sons—and fast!

But Merewyn, the stubborn lass, refuses to marry him and won't tell him why. Rocque can't imagine spending his life with anyone else! So if he can't marry another lass, and the one he wants won't marry him, what chance does he have to secure the title of the new laird?

As the Oliphant healer, Merewyn knows her value to the clan. She is also quite aware she doesn't *need* to marry...and the only way she will, is for love. And Rocque, stubborn idiot that he is, won't tell her his true feelings. Can she be blamed for saying *nay* to his proposal? But now she's running out of time and knows she has no choice but to tell him the truth, or set him free, because in a few months, everyone in the clan will know her secret!

Rocque might have more brawn than brains, but he's smart enough to know he can't lose Merewyn. But is he prepared for the battle it's going to take to prove that to her?

Warning: This story contains naughty bits. Lots of them. *Ridiculous* amounts. Also contains characters and conversations which are funny enough to make you spit out your tea. For the sake of your Kindle, do not drink while reading this book. That is all; you may now carry on.

OTHER BOOKS BY CAROLINE LEE

Want the scoop on new books? Join Caroline's Cohort, an exclusive reader group! Or sign up for my mailing list by texting "Caroline" to 42828 to get started!

Steamy Scottish Historicals:
The Sinclair Jewels (4 books)
The Highland Angels (4 books)
The Hots for Scots (7 books)

Sensual Historical Westerns:
Black Aces (3 books)
Sunset Valley (3 books)
Everland Ever After (10 books)
The Sweet Cheyenne Quartet (6 books)

Sweet Contemporary Westerns
Quinn Valley Ranch (5 books)
River's End Ranch (14 books)
The Cowboys of Cauldron Valley (3+ books)

Click **here** to find a complete list of Caroline's books.

*Sign up for Caroline's Newsletter to receive exclusive content and freebies, as well as first dibs on her books! Or if newsletters aren't your thing, follow her on **Bookbub** for a quick, concise new release alert every time she publishes a book!*

Dedication:
For Nancy, who will like the sexy bits.
And for Ellis, whose turnip obsession became useful in chapter eight.

PROLOGUE

THERE WAS something about waking up in a woman's bed, knowing the sheets were all clean and smelling fresh, and there'd be something warm to break his fast before long. But 'twas not just *any* woman who made Rocque smile when he opened his eyes.

'Twas Merewyn, and only Merewyn.

Grinning, he rolled over and propped himself up on his elbow. She was stretched out beside him, limbs akimbo, the coverlet kicked down around her waist and one of her red curls stuck in the dried drool beside her mouth. As he watched, she grunted and shifted position, as if personally affronted by the pillow.

She was beautiful.

He loved the way she could be as stubborn as he was, unwilling to settle for anything less than what she knew was the best. And as the Oliphant healer, Merewyn *often* knew what was best.

For everyone else, at least.

Rocque's smile slowly faded as he remembered the night before. They'd made love, and he'd asked—yet again—for her hand in marriage.

And yet again, she turned him down.

St. John's tits, but she was stubborn. And hot-headed. And difficult when she wouldn't just accept that she didn't know *everything* about *everything*. Their arguments had gotten to be legendary in the clan.

His lips curled upward once more. Their making-up had become legendary as well.

She had a way of distracting him from their disagreements which was the envy of every Oliphant warrior, he was certain.

But she was *his*.

Gently, he placed his large hand against her stomach, and when she didn't move, spread his fingers across her skin. He could imagine her swelling with his bairn, caring for them the way she cared for the villagers. They could be *happy* here together, in this little cottage.

She murmured something, and his gaze darted up to her face, but her eyes were still closed. And his lips twitched upward once more.

He'd been with her for almost a year. They'd spent the long winter keeping one another warm here in this very bed. He knew what she liked, and knew she liked what *he* liked.

Like mutual morning *likings*, for one thing.

Slowly, sneakily, he shifted until he was lying beside her, his body stretched out along hers, and his manhood already aching. She smelled of rosemary—the way she always did.

'Twas his favorite scent.

Mayhap the movement woke her, because she rolled toward him and opened her eyes.

They laid like that, their heads sharing the same pillow, gazing at one another.

He knew the moment she blinked away all the sleep, the moment she realized his unspoken suggestion.

Her brow twitched. "Good morning, lover."

He lifted himself up on one elbow, looming over her, and her lips stretched lazily to match his. As he lowered his lips, she reached one arm up to pull him closer.

A good morning, indeed.

CHAPTER 1

EVEN AT THE best of times, Oliphant Castle could be chaotic. But the great hall just prior to the midday meal? "Chaos" was being polite.

Rocque, the Oliphant commander and one of the laird's sons, frowned as he descended the stairs with his brother. Alistair was still talking, but Rocque's eyes darted across the hustle and bustle, ensuring there was order hidden among the turmoil.

Aye, there was Moira, the plump, middle aged housekeeper. She ran Oliphant Castle with an iron fist, and today was no different. As she appeared from the steps leading down to the kitchens, she was waving a long spoon and hollering orders to the servants and warriors who were helping to arrange the trestle tables and benches.

Satisfied, Rocque turned his attention back to his brother, who was saying something about... Wait, was he doing *maths*?

"So, by my calculations, we'll be using fewer resources and the men will be more alert if we switch to a rotation of three men every three hours, instead of two men every two hours."

Rocque's frown deepened as they reached the main floor and he lifted his hands from where they'd been resting on his sword belt.

Let's see. Three men, every three hours.

He held up three fingers, then six, then nine, whispering as he counted. When he reached twelve—and ran out of fingers—he switched back to zero fingers.

Versus two men every two hours.

Two fingers, then four, then six... He muttered names aloud, working through the evening watch rotation.

Finally, he shook out his fingers. With a scowl, he glanced at his brother.

"Ye ken math is no' my strong suit. But would we no' use the same number of men, even with that rotation?"

Alistair had been distracted by something across the hall, but when he glanced back, he offered Rocque a quick grin. "Aye, ye are correct. But 'twould mean the same men dinnae have to stand watch as often. Ye could push the rotation out to once a sennight, if ye include me and Malcolm more regularly."

Rocque's brows shot up and he regarded his brother. "Ye really are willing to stand guard again?"

Alistair wasn't one to shirk his duty to the clan. In fact, as near as Rocque could tell, Alistair's entire *life* revolved around duty to his clan. But the man spent most of his days in Da's solar, picking through letters and contracts and—Rocque shuddered—*maths*. In appreciation, when Rocque made the guard roster, he often left this brother of his off... Let him use his brain for the clan, while others— like Rocque—would use their muscles.

But Alistair slapped him on the shoulder with a grin. "Aye, brother. And dinnae think we havenae noticed ye leaving Malcolm off more'n a few times."

"Och, Malcolm's the smartest among us, but he's nae swordsman."

It wasn't disloyal to his twin for Rocque to say such a thing; he assured himself. Malcolm knew how to hold a sword, the same as all of William Oliphant's bastard sons. But he was the inventor of the group.

And besides, he'd worried over Rocque often enough that Rocque was more than willing to allow him his sleep when possible.

"Are ye speaking about me?"

Rocque and Alistair whirled to find their twins strolling toward them. Malcolm shared the same coloring with Rocque, although that's where their similarities ended. Alistair and Kiergan looked more alike than not, although their personalities were like cheese and chalk.

While Malcolm was focused on them, Kiergan was walking backward, flirting with one of the serving wenches who blushed prettily at his winks.

Although Rocque had seen this brother of theirs balance along the keep's battlements blindfolded, he was tempted to shove a foot in Kiergan's path in irritation.

"Aye," Alistair drawled, responding to Mal. "Rocque was telling me how much he admires yer swordsmanship."

Their scholarly brother blinked. "Did ye hit yer head, Rocque?" He held up three fingers. "How many fingers do ye see? Are things blurry?"

Knowing his twin was only half teasing, Rocque scowled. "I'm putting ye on the roster *twice* in the next sennight, Alistair!"

Kiergan had finally decided to join them and settled into an easy stance beside his twin. "Rocque's putting together the roster? Any chance I could have off tonight? I have a…" He glanced over at the serving lass, Minnie. "I'm hoping to be busy."

"What ye do on yer own time is yer own business. I'll no' adjust the roster because ye cannae manage to keep yer cock tucked where it belongs."

"Where it belongs is up for some debate."

Rocque groaned as Alistair rolled his eyes.

But Malcolm smirked. "When yer commander tells ye it belongs in yer kilt, Minnie's opinion matters less."

"But *my commander* is the one who is always telling me to practice my swordplay!" Kiergan protested.

Alistair pinched the bridge of his nose, and Rocque burst out, "By St. John's bollocks, not *everything* is a cock joke, Kiergan!"

This rakish brother of theirs merely smiled. "Then ye're no' trying hard enough."

Malcolm nodded; his expression too innocent to be believed. " 'Tis what she said."

Kiergan's mouth dropped open and his twin burst into surprised laughter.

Rocque wasn't too far behind. "*What* is that supposed to mean?"

Their scholarly brother shrugged as he launched into a long-winded explanation. " 'Hard enough' seemed like prime opportunity to make another cock joke. So I merely referenced what, say, Minnie, might be thinking when it came to Kiergan's dick being hard enough—"

The rest of his explanation was drowned out by Rocque and Alistair's laughter, but Kiergan seemed excited.

" *'Tis what she said*," he repeated. "I like it! I think ye'd discovered a new joke, brother. There's a limited number of new jokes in the world, ye ken." He clasped Malcolm on the shoulder. "Generations from now, men will be calling one another's manhood into question with shouts of *'Tis what she said!*"

Malcolm nodded. "Imagine the possibilities!" He gestured gallantly. "*Pardon, fine sir, but could ye help me work on my swordplay?*"

" 'Tis what she said!" Kiergan replied, chortling.

Straightening, Malcolm held his palms facing one another, shoulder width apart. "*Ye should've seen it! I've never caught one so big.*"

" 'Tis what she said!"

Rocque's laughter had died down, but his grin was still there when he chimed it. "*Aye, big and slippery!*"

" 'Tis what she said!" Mal joined Kiergan in the refrain.

Alistair shook his head, but was smiling. "*Thick and slimy, and smelled of fish!*"

" 'Tis what she— Wait." Kiergan frowned at his twin. "I'm no' sure ye understand the mechanics of this joke."

"Either the mechanics of this joke, or the mechanics of sexual congress," Malcolm muttered to Kiergan. "Want me to take him aside and have a talk with him?"

"Oh, for fook's sake!" Alistair threw his hands up in exasperation, but he was still grinning when he continued, "For that, ye're all heading to the wall with me this afternoon to work on the reinforcing."

Kiergan shrugged. " 'Twas my plan. I have to keep my muscles toned *somehow*, if I want to keep impressing the lasses."

"Going to flab, eh?" Rocque nodded thoughtfully. "Alistair, remind me to add him to the roster twice next week as well."

"Thank ye," Kiergan breathed with reverence, as he clasped his hands to his heart. "Just what I was hoping for. I *love* to work to the point of exhaustion, especially if 'tis hard."

" 'Tis what she said," Alistair muttered.

As Rocque snorted, his twin nodded.

"I'll head down to the smithy after the meal," Malcolm said with excitement. "Duncan and his stepfather were working on one of the pulleys I modified for the lifting mechanism."

Alistair lifted a brow in Rocque's direction. "Have ye seen Malcolm's latest invention to get the stones up from the bailey? 'Twill significantly cut down on how much manpower we require."

Shaking his head, Rocque didn't bother hiding his grin. "Why bother? Just send Kiergan up to show off his *manpower*."

Malcolm solemnly intoned, " 'Tis what she said."

"Aright, ye lot!" Kiergan burst out, "ye've killed it. Ye murdered the joke with overuse. Amazing that ye can create and destroy a joke in such a short amount of time! Ye'd think such a thing would be hard, but nay!"

" 'Tis what she—"

"*Shut it,* Alistair!"

Chuckling now, Rocque held up his hand to halt the bickering. "Nay, I have nae seen Mal's newest creation, and aye, I'll be up there to help. I promised the lads I'd join them on the lists later this afternoon." The youngest of the Oliphant warriors sometimes requested extra sparring sessions with him after the morning practice was done. "But I can help prior to that."

He'd been *hoping* to spend an hour or two at home, but being a part of a clan meant sacrifices.

Besides, 'twas not as if the little cottage where he'd been hoping to visit was actually *home.*

It just felt that way.

Technically, as the commander, he had a chamber in the barracks all to himself. 'Twas a simple room, but more than enough for a man like him.

But over the last year, many of his belongings had migrated into the village, to a cozy cottage set back off the main square and surrounded by the most extensive herb garden he'd ever seen.

The cottage belonged to Merewyn, the Oliphant healer. The woman he—well, he cared for her, certainly. He enjoyed spending time with her. He valued her insights and the way she made him feel when she fussed over him.

And St. John knew he loved the way they made love.

In fact, thinking of how he'd woken her that morning—with a smile and a raging erection she was glad to see—his cock twitched again under his kilt.

Aye, mayhap he *had* been hoping to sneak away to that cozy little cottage and spend some time with her, if it wasn't too hard.

He silently snorted to himself. *'Tis what she said.*

His brothers were still ribbing one another, but Rocque just smiled as he let their bickering and teasing wash over him. He and Malcolm had joined this household when they were lads of twelve, but that still meant he'd spent more than half his life with Finn and Duncan, Alistair and Kiergan.

And--his gaze swept the hall—Moira and Da and most of the clanmembers here. Three years ago, when Da had made him commander, Rocque had taken over the training of the Oliphant warriors, and had gotten to know all these men better.

There were some—like Fergus and Allan, whom he nodded to across the hall—who were older than he was, and although it was his job to train, he respected their skills, knowledge and experience. Then there were the lads he was scheduled to work with that after-noon, who werenae too much older than he'd been when he arrived, but eager to prove themselves as warriors.

Aye, most of the men under his command settled neatly into their roles. Only a few still gave him trouble.

His lips pulled down as he saw one of those troublemakers lingering near the stairs to the kitchens. Hamish was the same age as Rocque and his brothers, so they'd been thrown together more than once growing up. It had become clear then, and was more so now, that Hamish was one of those men who was good at making excuses. Things were never his fault, or were accidents, or someone else was to blame. The man was a terrible warrior, but never bothered to work to overcome his shortcomings.

In fact, when Da had handed the role of commander over to Rocque, the old man had smiled grimly and pointed to Hamish. "Ye'll have yer hands full figuring out what to do with that one," he'd said, and he'd been right.

And since, when confronted, Hamish did little but whine about life's fairness, Rocque was always at a loss for how to punish the man. Challenging him with the sword didn't work, and the man wouldn't raise his fists, because he knew Rocque was twice his size.

Stifling a sigh, Rocque watched Hamish's eyes light up as he straightened and darted forward. Who was he waiting on—? Ah.

The lassie who emerged from the kitchens wasn't who Rocque had expected. For one thing, she was young—Jessie was only thirteen, as he recalled. Mayhap not even that. He wracked his brain, trying to recall if Hamish was connected to Jessie's family in any way. Judging from the way the man dogged her steps, 'twas clear he was trying to speak to her.

And from the way she tucked her chin against her chest, kept her eyes on her tray of flagons, and hurried for the trestle tables, 'twas clear she was trying to avoid him.

Hmm.

When Hamish said one more thing to the lassie, then did something which caused her to jump and blush, Rocque's frown grew. At last Hamish sauntered off, smirking, but what had he said to wee Jessie?

The girl was a new addition to the keep. Over the years, servants had come and gone; mostly lasses from the village who married and moved away. Sometimes they stayed after marriage, if their husbands lived in the village and they needed the coin. And sometimes they stayed because they made homes for themselves here in the Castle.

Jessie was—or would be—one of the latter. She'd only joined the household a few months ago, as he recalled. She'd been the only child of a crofter whose wife was long gone. In late winter, their croft had burned. Her father had been trapped, and although she'd fought to free him, the older man had perished.

The poor lass had been left with naught but her burns—terrible things which covered one arm and half her face—and her night terrors. Merewyn had been up at the keep often in those first months, caring for the girl and soothing her. Jessie still didn't speak much, from what Rocque had heard, and the lass didn't deserve to be pestered by the likes of Hamish.

The knowledge Rocque *couldn't* pound some sense into Hamish— because the wee shite wouldn't meet him on the lists, instead whining about Rocque's size being *unfair*—had his hands curling into fists at his side. St. John's knuckles! Rocque needed to pound on something.

Mayhap later he could visit the bag and pretend 'twas Hamish as he slammed his fists into it. 'Twas a useful training tool, and handy for getting out his frustration, especially over one of his men he couldn't punch directly.

"So, what do ye think, Rocque?"

Alistair's question startled him out of his thoughts, and he turned his frown to his brothers. "What?"

"Och, I told ye he wasnae interested," Kiergan said dismissively.

" 'Tis what she said," Malcolm muttered.

Rocque rolled his eyes. "Are ye speaking of something relevant, or can I go back to my musings?"

Kiergan flicked his fingers. "Completely irrelevant. Alistair was trying to convince me to woo a lass for him to marry, and Malcolm was explaining how we were all going about it incorrectly."

"Ye are," Malcolm defended. "If ye want to be laird, ye need—"

"I dinnae," Kiergan interrupted flatly.

Earlier that summer, Da had collected his six illegitimate sons and explained that since they all had fine qualities befitting the future Laird Oliphant, and because they were all so close in age, there wasn't a clear choice of who to declare his heir.

Therefore, the easiest way to make the decision would be to grant the position to whichever son had an heir of his own.

All six Oliphant bastards had to marry, and the first one to produce a son would become the next laird.

Of course, the fact that not all his sons *wanted* the position didn't seem to bother William Oliphant. Kiergan, for instance, still laughed whenever someone brought up the idea of *him* succeeding his father.

Alistair declared himself too busy to find a wife, and Malcolm had decided the way to become the next laird was to find a widow with a "proven history of successfully baring sons." He was still searching for a suitable candidate.

And Rocque? Well, Rocque had already found the woman he wanted to marry.

Now he just had to convince her.

Speaking of lovers...

Rocque quickly lost interest in his brother's arguments again when he saw a flash of purple at the top of the stone stairs. He would recognize that gown anywhere; 'twas his favorite!

Sure enough, 'twas Merewyn who hurried down the stairs, her skirts in one hand and her basket in the other. She must've been tending to Aunt Agatha in her chambers—the old woman had complained about her gout acting up again.

Stepping away from his brothers, and not giving two shites if they thought him rude—Rocque met Merewyn at the bottom of the stairs. They were surrounded by their clan, and she was obviously in a hurry, but when she saw him her expression lit up and she dropped her skirts to reach for his hand.

He used that hold to pull her into an embrace. Their kiss was hard and fast, just enough to remind her she belonged with him.

Just enough to leave *him* wanting more.

"Hello, Rocque," she said with a breathless grin as he released her.

Stepping back, she tried to smooth the bodice of her gown, and he grinned.

"Where are ye off to in such a hurry? Will ye stay and dine with us?"

As he asked, he gestured to the hall. Moira and Cook always made sure there was enough at the noon meal to accommodate anyone who wanted to join them, with plenty of leftovers for stragglers throughout the afternoon or to take to clanmembers who couldn't participate for whatever reason.

"Thank ye," she said with a pretty smile, even as she shook her head. "But Megan has invited me to sup with her and her husband today. She's near to burst with that bairn of hers, and I think it's important to give her things to focus on besides the coming birth."

Nodding, Rocque shrugged to let her know he didn't begrudge her absence. Merewyn was an important member of the Oliphant clan, and as healer and midwife, she was always in demand.

He glanced over at wee Jessie, who was now laying out a large serving bowl on one of the tables. It looked like 'twould be a simple meal; Cook often made stew to serve atop a bland, piping hot porridge. The stew could be allowed to sit, and as long as the simple porridge was made fresh, the diners would be satisfied.

"If Megan makes a better meal, mayhap I'll join ye," he teased.

With a grin, she swatted his arm, then turned the movement into a caress even as she stepped away. "I promise ye mutton for tonight. Is that acceptable?"

"Aye, lass." He winked. "I'll likely be hungry."

And he didn't just mean because of the afternoon's work.

When she blushed happily like that, her red curls blended with her skin, and her gray eyes twinkled. She stretched herself up on her toes —and it was a stretch, because she was so much smaller than he—and brushed a kiss across his cheek.

"I'll be waiting," she murmured.

Then she picked up her skirts and hurried out of the hall, calling greetings to those she passed.

Rocque wasn't the only one to watch her go. She was well-loved, and most of the Oliphants smiled when they waved to her.

Hamish, however, just glared.

I need to figure out what's going on there.

Rocque knew he wasn't the sharpest tool in the smithy, but if he couldn't work out the problem with his brain, he could always use his fists.

He was still mulling over the dilemma when he sat down to eat, the porridge steaming in his trencher even before he poured the stew over and reached for a spoon.

"Yer brother just told me a joke."

His father's voice was quieter than normal, which is how Rocque knew he was looking for a private conversation. Instead of announcing his presence jovially, the younger man shifted down on the bench to make room for his father to join him.

He didn't even have to ask which brother. "Did it involve fish or swords?"

Da snorted as he settled himself. "This one involved swords, although judging by the use of ' *'tis what she said,*' it was supposed to be a metaphor."

"Kiergan claims Mal has invented humor."

Nodding, the older man reached for a flagon of ale. "The lad is *good* at inventing. Ye're good at leading."

It always made Rocque vaguely uncomfortable—in a good way—when Da began to praise him with his way with the men. Rocque *knew* he was a good leader, and appreciated that his father had given him the opportunity. But being *praised* for it was another thing entirely.

Most fathers were stingy with their praises. Hell, the only father-figure Rocque and Malcolm had had as lads was their mother's distant relative, who'd used them all as drudges and beaten Mam to death.

But Da was different. Not only did he care about all of his children—not just his sons, but Nessa, his only child from his only marriage—but he'd gone out of his way to find and gather all six of his bastards under one roof. Where he'd raised them with bluster, patience, humor, and quite a lot of help from Moira.

And his sons loved him for it. Rocque knew they all—even flippant Kiergan—would walk through the fires of Hell itself for the man.

Da had obviously been thinking of something else. "Aye, Malcolm has a brain in his head, 'tis for certain. His scheme to find a wife is a good one." He paused, the spoon halfway to his lips, and hit Rocque with a raised brow. "How is yers coming along?"

Ah. Da wanted to talk *marriage*.

Sighing, Rocque reached for his ale. Of all the Oliphant bastards, he looked most like their father. He and Malcolm shared the man's russet hair and blue eyes, although Rocque was the one to share his size. Of course, Da's beard was shot through with more gray than Rocque's, who kept his trim, but 'twas obvious they were father and son.

So why in all that's holy would my father *call me out like that?*

What had he just been thinking about his father caring? Rocque snorted quietly.

Figuring he'd stalled all he could, he finally said, "My scheme's going fine, Da."

'Twas only a little lie, and mayhap the older man sensed that.

"So, if things are going so *fine* between ye and Merewyn, when are ye going to ask her to be yer bride, lad? She's no' of high birth, but neither are ye, truthfully. She's no' only an Oliphant—and dinnae think I dinnae appreciate the idea of yer loyalties no' being divided by yer wife's family—but a valued member of the clan. A healer! Ye cannae sniff at a wife with that status, lad."

Frowning down at his ale, Rocque tried to make sense of his father's meaning.

I ken what a double negative is, but how many times did the old man say "not"?

"Well?" Apparently Da was tired of giving him time to think.

Sighing, Rocque had to admit to his father, "I've asked her."

"Ye've asked Merewyn to marry ye?"

Why did the old man sound so surprised? "Aye," Rocque offered hesitantly.

William Oliphant frowned. "And the lass turned ye down?" When Rocque didn't respond—his answer should be obvious, after all—the laird slammed down his flagon. "She turned *ye* down? Who in the hell does she think she is? She cannae just break the heart of one of my sons and go on—"

"Da," Rocque shifted to face his father fully, concerned by the way the older man's face was turning red. "*Da*, calm down. She has a right to say nae to me or any man. All women do—ye raised us that way."

"But—but no' when it comes to marriage!"

Would it be rude to roll his eyes? Aye, likely.

"Da, she is her own woman and can deny a marriage suit if she chooses." Even if he didn't understand why. "But I havenae given up asking her."

Just have to find a way to make her see how good *life could be, were we married.*

There was a part of him though, a worried part, which had been growing since the first time she'd said *nay*, which wondered if mayhap she saw their relationship differently than he did.

For the last year, he'd been content with their affair. Waking up with her, breaking his fast with her, spending his evenings with her... that was how he imagined married life with her.

But why didn't she share that dream?

Da was frowning at him. "How many times have ye asked her?"

Rocque shrugged. "A few times." And he'd ask her again, until she either said *aye*, or gave him an explanation.

His father appeared calmer now. When he exhaled, the older man's shoulders slumped slightly, and he dug his spoon into his meal.

"Well, mayhap 'tis for the best."

Well *that* was a surprise.

"What?" he blurted.

Da refused to look at him. "I said, mayhap 'tis for the best. Mayhap the lass is doing it for ye."

Frowning now, Rocque pushed his own trencher away. His stomach had soured in worry. "What are ye saying?"

William Oliphant sighed, his blue eyes darting to his son's, then away once more. "The challenge I set before ye lads is nae secret, Rocque," he said almost gently. "Mayhap Merewyn kens what ye need to do to become laird, and is making sure ye get it."

Rocque *knew* he wasn't as smart as some of his brothers...hell, there were likely *sheep* smarter than he was. But why couldn't he understand what his father meant?

"In order to become laird," he began slowly, "I need a wife and a son. I'm working on getting the wife."

"And as I've heard it, lad, ye've been working on getting the bairn for nigh a year now."

Still frowning in confusion, Rocque glanced at his father.

Who was...*blushing*?

By St. John's warts, what was going on here?

"Aye, she's been my woman for the last twelve-month."

Finally, his father met his eyes, still fiddling with his spoon. "And if ye've been fooking her for a year, lad, why has she no' fallen pregnant? Mayhap she *cannae*. She's the village midwife, aye? Mayhap she kens she's barren, and 'tis why she's denying yer suit."

Across the hall, one voice called out for more porridge. Another answered, and then the hum of conversation faded as Rocque's throat forgot how to work.

Mayhap she kens she's barren.

Was Merewyn barren?

His father was right. They'd spent the last year enjoying one another's bodies in the most perfect way...and she'd never missed her cycle. Had she?

Maths weren't his strong suit, but surely he would've noticed?

He blew out a breath. His father was right. In a year, he hadn't gotten Merewyn with child. If she *couldn't* become pregnant, was *that* the reason she was denying his marriage proposal?

He forced himself to breathe, to focus on the light coming in through the high windows across the hall. He could no longer hear the hubbub from his clan eating, but it mattered not...because his own pulse was hammering in his temples so strongly, he couldn't make sense of his own thoughts.

St. John's tits, was his father right? Was Merewyn barren?

Resting atop the table, his hand involuntarily curled into a fist around the spoon. Just this morning, she'd ridden him as if he were an untamed stallion and she some kind of—of—well, he couldn't think of the right analogy.

Or was it a metaphor?

Either way, she fooked him cross-eyed, and after he'd held her and thanked all the saints in Heaven for giving him such a blessed life.

If she was barren, surely she would've told him so?

Or was Da right, and *this* was the reason she kept refusing to marry him?

Swallowing, he forced his heartbeat—and reaction—under control. When he glanced over, his father was still eating. But the look in his identical blue eyes was expectant, like he was waiting for Rocque to deny the possibility.

He couldn't.

Da's bushy brows dipped down. "Och, lad, I'm sorry." He straightened with a sigh and tossed down his spoon. "She's a good lass. Mayhap—"

Both of their attention was caught by a shout. They both turned toward the argument going on at the center table. Brohn, Moira's eldest, was standing with his hands fisted in front of him as he glared across the table at Hamish. The smaller man was smirking as he gestured, while Brohn's face was turning red. The men around them were calling out, but 'twas impossible to hear individual words.

But Brohn was level-headed, which was something Rocque had always admired about the younger man. He was quiet and thought things through before speaking, and the men admired his quiet certainty. Rocque had been considering making Brohn his second, and judging from the way the men were supporting the younger man, 'twould be a good move.

At the other tables, men and women both were either ignoring the ruckus, or peering around companions to get a closer look. Across the way, a warrior lifted his hand to beckon for another helping, and Rocque saw Jessie nod and lift the pot of steaming porridge before hurrying toward the diner.

"She's my sister, ye bastard!" Brohn roared, and Rocque saw Kiergan lurch forward. This rakish brother of theirs would never allow Lara to be insulted, and of them, he was the closest with her brother Brohn.

Before Da could respond, Rocque had shoved himself to his feet. "Cease!" he bellowed.

His command gained the attention of Brohn and most of the men at his table, but Hamish continued to wave his hands as he explained his joke. He swept one arm around behind him expansively, just as Jessie rushed by.

The back of his hand caught her under her burden, and Rocque knew he wasn't the only one in the hall to hold his breath as the piping-hot, sticky porridge flew up into Jessie's face.

The first sound the girl made was a kind of gurgle—the porridge was thick as tar, and just as hot—but by the time the pot hit the floor and she reached for her face, she was screaming.

High-pitched, frantic screams.

Poor lass must've been reminded of the pain from her burns, which had only just healed.

Cursing, Rocque leapt across the table, intent on helping. By the time he reached them, Moira and Minnie were already bent over the poor girl, doing their best to calm her agonized screams. So he turned his anger where it belonged.

Hamish took one look at Rocque and began backing away. " 'Twas an accident! How was I to ken the clumsy lass was standing behind me like that?"

Typical Hamish; shifting the blame. Fists clenched, Rocque stalked forward. "Ye were the one to start the argument..."

"Bah!" Hamish almost tripped over a stool, but quickly righted himself. "Brohn cannae take a joke, 'tis all. I cannae be blamed for the girl's clumsiness or his inability to—"

Rocque was done.

Without breaking stride, he hauled back and slammed a fist into Hamish's nose. There was a satisfying *crunch* and the man went down without a whimper.

Rocque stared at the unconscious man a moment, cradling his fist, then spat. "Actually, ye can be blamed for much more than ye think, Hamish."

When the murmurs and cheers began around him, he whirled back to find Jessie's screams had turned to tears. In two strides he was at her side, nudging Moira out of the way.

"Minnie, see to the rest of the meal, aye? Moira, fetch cloths and clean water." With barely a grunt, he rose to his feet, cradling the sobbing lass against his chest.

He made eye contact with Brohn, who had a disgusted expression on his face. "Fetch Merewyn, and tell her to bring her herbs." Not that the woman went anywhere without them. "We'll be in the kitchens."

His friend nodded, before stepping over the bench, spitting on Hamish, and hurrying off.

Rocque glanced at Moira, but the housekeeper was already heading for the kitchens. She stopped to exchange a look with the laird, and Da nodded as he rose to his feet and followed.

Cradling the crying lass in his arms, Rocque headed for the kitchens, aching for her pain.

CHAPTER 2

MEREWYN HURRIED THROUGH THE VILLAGE, her skirts held high in one hand while she juggled her supplies in the other. She was following Brohn, whose long legs made it difficult for someone of her size to keep up with him.

"The porridge landed across her face, neck, and chest," the young man was calling over his shoulder to her as they headed for the keep. "Ye ken how sticky it can be."

She winced, praying she'd brought enough goatweed. Poor Jessie had been through so much pain in the last few months; it didn't seem fair to inflict her with more. *Especially* not more burns.

"Do ye ken if the skin had blistered?"

But Brohn just shrugged, stepping to one side at the bottom of the steps and waiting for her to catch up. "She was still covered in the stuff as Rocque took her to the kitchens and started bellowing orders. But 'twas only a few moments ago, Healer. 'Tis lucky I caught ye afore ye left for Megan's home."

Only a few moments.

Well, thank the Virgin for small blessings.

Nodding distractedly, Merewyn hurried past him on her way into the great hall. As Brohn had said, half the diners were still eating, while more were whispering to one another. Or gesturing as they'd relived what had happened. Brohn had told her of Hamish's actions, and she was pleased to see the weasel of a man had recovered enough to drag himself away before she'd arrived.

There's no telling if she'd have the discipline *not* to spit on him as she passed.

Already mentally cataloguing what was in her basket, Merewyn hurried past them all on her way to the kitchen stairs. She'd need hemlock for pain, and goatweed for the burns, assuming the skin hadn't broken as badly as last time.

Nae use borrowing trouble. Ye'll see what's what soon enough.

She found them all in the little room behind the hearth, where Cook usually slept. Merewyn's eyes went right to the bed, and not just because poor Jessie was still sniffling. Nay, 'twas the man beside the lass, the huge man, who was gently resting the girl against the pillows, who made her heart beat faster.

Blessed Virgin, but how could he still have this effect on her? Merewyn's hand dropped to her stomach, in a futile effort to ease the little flip-flopping Rocque's gaze always caused her. He had the most wonderfully intense blue eyes, set in a wide face framed by russet hair which was always in need of a trim. Today his hair hung in his eyes, and she vowed to talk him into letting her trim it soon.

When he straightened, Rocque sent a glance her way, and she swore she saw relief—and something else?—in his gaze before he nodded. The command in that one movement told her he'd never doubted she'd arrive.

And why wouldn't she? This was her life, after all.

She was a healer, and at her clan's beck and call.

Even if she'd rather belong to just one man.

This man.

On the bed, Jessie gave a little whimper, and Merewyn snapped herself out of her fanciful wishes and hurried forward.

"Well, let us see what kind of damage has been—*Och*, ye're still covered in it!"

From her side of the bed, she glared up at Rocque. "Ye dinnae even think to clean the poor lass?"

He raised a brow at her censure, and one side of his lips twitched. "I've been *busy*."

She clucked her tongue as she turned back to the girl. "Well, at least ye mopped some of it off with yer shirt." The front of his linen shirt was caked in porridge, and she hoped *he* hadn't been burned as well. "But now we have to clean the rest."

"Here, lass, I'll help."

The offer came from Moira, who ran the Oliphant keep with an iron fist, and was rumored to have helped raise Rocque's brothers the same way. She'd just stepped into the small room with the laird, who crossed his arms and rested his shoulder against the door jamb as he watched them work.

Nay he watched *Moira*, and wasn't that interesting?

Merewyn shook her head to focus. "Are yer hands clean?"

The older woman was well-rounded, with a kind face which was now pinched with concern as she held out a cloth. "Always," she declared indignantly.

Hiding her smile, Merewyn quickly folded a cloth and dunked it in the bowl of cool, clear water. "First we need to wipe it off." She gave Jessie a gentle smile. "I ken it hurts, lassie, but can ye be brave for us?"

When the girl whimpered, Moira clucked pityingly and nudged Merewyn aside as she leaned forward to gently clean the porridge from Jessie's face and neck.

Stepping back, Merewyn watched the housekeeper critically for a moment, then nodded in approval. 'Twas obvious from the concern in the older woman's gaze that she cared about the girl. Since Jessie's arrival at Oliphant Castle, she'd likely been in Moira's care, and there was no doubt the lass needed love and affection.

Even more so, now.

Merewyn glanced toward the door, only to see the laird's wistful look as he gazed at the pair on the bed. Her eyes widened slightly, but Rocque's quiet question cut through her musings.

"What do ye need?"

"Um…" She stepped toward a small table and upended her basket. "Cold water, lots of it. As cold as possible. I'll see what else…"

She trailed off as she began to paw through her herbs, dimly aware of Rocque's nod.

But it was his father who spoke up. "I'll get it. Well," he added with a chuckle, "I'll have Minnie organize it. But ye'll have yer cold water, Healer."

Nodding distractedly, she murmured her thanks as she felt, more than heard, Rocque move up behind her. Her fingers didn't need her brain's interference as they deftly sorted through the herbs she'd need for this afternoon's work, so she glanced up at him.

Dear Lord in Heaven, but those eyes! Her stomach flipped over again, at the way those blue-gray depths swirled with emotion. She saw anger there, aye, but also…sorrow?

"What happened?" she whispered, not wanting to disturb the pair on the bed.

Rocque didn't seem as concerned with niceties. "Hamish," he growled.

Well, that was no more than she knew already. Frowning, Merewyn settled her hip against the table and raised her brows, urging him to continue. "Hamish hit her, Brohn said."

When he crossed his arms in front of his chest, it pulled the material of his shirt, and she noticed yet again just how much porridge covered him. Thanks to his quick action to bring Jessie to the kitchens, that shirt would need to be washed before it was ruined.

With a sigh, he scrubbed his hand across his face. "The idiot is an expert at shifting the blame. I am no' sure if 'twas an accident as he claimed."

"But ye hit him?" According to Brohn, at least.

Frowning, Rocque stared down at his knuckles. "Aye," he admitted. "I should no' have, since he's so much smaller than me. I've resisted the urge for years—and believe me, he tries my patience." Still rubbing at the back of his hand, he glanced up at her. "But 'twas his *reaction* to it I couldnae abide, Mere," he hissed, his eyes darting to the bed and back. "The lass was lying there screaming in pain, and he refused to acknowledge his fault!"

Mayhap *this* accounted for the sorrow she'd seen in his eyes.

Blowing out a breath, she patted him on the knuckles, then wrapped her fingers around his and gave them a squeeze. "From what I ken of Hamish, lover, he's needed a good head-knocking."

He lifted another brow at her claim, and she shrugged. "He's a bit of a shite-weasel, is he no'?"

Merewyn hadn't lived in the village her whole life, but she was an Oliphant, through and through. When she'd heard that the old Healer was ailing, she'd moved near the keep to take over caring for the people, and had gotten used to putting off men who were interested in her.

Interested in *having* her. Owning her.

Since aligning with Rocque, the rest of the warriors had stopped pestering her...all but one. Hamish had, more than once, found her alone and struck up a conversation. It had all been innocent, but struck her as wrong.

"When did he speak with ye?" Rocque growled.

She shrugged, dropping his hand and turning her attention back to her herbs. "Sometimes he speaks *at* me. I dinnae encourage him, but I am no' rude either."

At first, he'd tried to manipulate her into spending time with him, but she was no fool, and quickly saw through his schemes. But she'd kept an eye on him, because there were plenty of lasses who *would* fall for his manipulations and insults hidden as clever compliments.

"What do ye speak of?"

Rocque had gentled his voice, although she could tell he was fighting a powerful emotion of some sort.

She rolled her eyes, more at his possessiveness than the thought of *Hamish* being a rival. "The weather, his prowess with a blade, and what a good kisser he is. The man likes to hear himself talk."

Come to think of it, Hamish had always wanted to speak of *himself*, which is why she avoided him when possible. His opinion of his own skills and bravery were tiring.

When Rocque blew out a breath, she glanced his way. He was shaking his head.

"I ken I shouldnae be jealous, Mere, but I am. Ye're my woman, and if I have my way, ye'll be my wife. The way he's always been sniffing around yer skirts..."

My woman.

She hadn't agreed to that. What they had was an informal arrangement, and he'd asked her to marry him. That would formalize things, but she...

She couldn't say yes.

Forcing a smile, she stretched up on her toes and planted a kiss on his cheek. "Then I guess 'tis best I'm no' yet *yer wife*, eh?"

Before he could do more than suck in a breath, Minnie bustled in with a pitcher of cold water. Merewyn nodded thankfully for the distraction and whirled toward the bed. "Let us see if those burns are clean!" she called in an over-loud voice.

Moira had done a thorough job, and Merewyn was able to examine the wound much easier now.

With sure movements, she made the whimpering lass a drink from a pinch of powdered hemlock mixed with water, and helped her sit up long enough to finish it.

" 'Twill ease the pain, and make my work easier." The drink would also make Jessie sleep deeply, which would help her heal.

She narrated her actions, more from habit than anything else. Over the years, she'd found that her patients—and their families—appreciated knowing what was going on. On the one hand, it would enable them to help themselves...and on the other, it made her actions less mysterious.

Many a healer has been accused of witchcraft because her patients didn't understand her potions.

Patients' potions. *Heh.*

"Och, well, 'tis no' so bad, lass," she murmured, turning Jessie's head to one side so she could brush her fingertips across the angry red welts. "Think of how much worse it would hurt if yer *hair* were caught against these burns, aye?"

The girl reacted to the humor in Merewyn's voice more than anything, and blew out a little breath which sounded it might be distantly related to a laugh. In the fire which had killed her father, Jessie had lost her hair. It had been burning when they'd pulled her free, and her rescuers had hacked it off to save her. Most days she wore a tam to cover the remaining wisps, but Merewyn and Moira both had assured her it *would* grow back.

Clucking her tongue soothingly, reached for a bowl and a pouch. "This is powdered goatweed, which ye should remember well, I'm sorry to say." Deftly, she pinched a bit into the bowl, and added some water, which she mixed with her fingertip. "See, I'll spread it across the burns, same as last time. Last time I mixed it with animal fat, because I needed it to stay longer, but those burns were much worse."

Soothingly, she kept up the narration as she moved across Jessie's face and neck. "Luckily, none of these burns have broken the skin, although this spot does bear watching."

She paid special attention to the hollow at the base of the girl's throat, where the skin was more inflamed. When Jessie hissed in pain, Merewyn reached for the cloth to dip into the pitcher of cold water.

"The goatweed will keep down the infection and pain, but I am sorry to say the best relief will simply be cold water. We can rotate out the wet cloths in order to give ye relief—"

"I'll take care of it, Healer." Moira jumped up, her plump hands already folding another cloth.

Nodding gratefully, Merewyn rose to her feet and stretched her back as she blew out a breath. Silently, she said a prayer of thanksgiving that Jessie's burns hadn't been worse. Truthfully, some of the scarring from her earlier burns had likely protected her today. 'Twas hard to tell, but it was possible her screams had been less from the heat from the porridge and more from the *memory* of the earlier pain.

Jessie's eyes were getting heavy, and Merewyn nodded as she collected her herbs. "Keep bathing her. Once she's asleep, just focus on the worst of it."

Moira didn't look up from her ministrations. "She'll sleep through the night again?"

" 'Tis likely." The hemlock was potent, even in the tiniest of doses. "Tomorrow, make sure she has plenty of water. And plenty of meat and leafy greens, to replenish her humors, aright?"

The housekeeper glanced up with a kind smile. "Meat, greens, humors. Got it."

"What's this I hear about an emergency?"

The strident call came from just outside the room, and as Merewyn turned, she caught Rocque's roll of his eyes. Luckily, by the time Lady Agatha had burst into the room, he'd controlled his expression. The dear old bat was the laird's aunt, and Rocque's great-aunt, but everyone in the keep referred to her as *Aunt Agatha*, and tolerated her histrionics.

"Ye had the bollocks to have an *emergency* without calling me?" she called angrily as she clumped into the room, her cane smacking against the floor in time with her wrapped foot.

"My apologies, Aunt," Rocque said blandly as he crossed to lend her an arm to rest on. "We were occupied and forgot about fetching ye for yer approval."

"Besides," Merewyn butted in, "ye're supposed to be elevating that foot."

"Bah!" The old woman waved her hand. "And miss out on the excitement?"

On the bed, Jessie made a little sound, and Moira turned to glare at them all. Taking control of the situation, Merewyn nodded to the housekeeper, then collected her herbs in her basket and shooed Rocque and his aunt out into the kitchen.

"Milady, 'twas merely a domestic accident," she whispered. "Not nearly as bad as the poor lass's previous burns, and she has been well-tended."

Lady Agatha had been one of her patients for years, and now the old woman peered suspiciously at Merewyn, half-supported by Rocque. "By *ye?*"

"Aye, milady. And Moira will ensure Jessie is cared for. I'll be back tomorrow to tend to her *and* yer foot, which ye really need to rest—"

"Nonsense. I came down for some porridge, but when I heard

what had happened, I'm nae longer hungry." Sniffing, the lady peered up at her great-nephew. "I can sit with Moira, and—*God's Nipples, lad!* Ye're covered in porridge!"

In a blink, she'd straightened out of Rocque's hold, proving she hadn't really needed him to hold her, and was patting at his arms— the highest on him she could reach.

"Were ye burned as well, lad? Do ye need my help?"

It was clear Rocque was trying to hide his smile—Merewyn didn't bother—when he gently caught hold of his aunt's slapping hands. "I'm fine, Agatha. 'Tis the porridge from Jessie's incident, and I barely noticed."

"Well, now I have to wash *my* hands." Agatha scowled down at the porridge on her palms. "Ye could've mentioned that *before* I got all concerned for ye, clot-heid."

"Sorry," Rocque said cheerfully.

Sniffing indignantly, Agatha straightened, and hobbled over to where she'd dropped her cane when she'd entered. Although her gout gave her trouble, Merewyn had long suspected the old woman only carried a cane to whack her great-nephews with occasionally.

Or often.

"Get yer arse over here, Rocque!" she scolded, "and escort me to the well so I can clean myself."

"Aye, Aunt. Since ye are clearly elderly and need my help, I'll—"

His teasing had the desired effect. With a curse, her cane caught him in the side of the leg. "I am *no'* elderly! I will go myself!"

Off she hobbled, muttering under her breath about indignities of age and rude upstarts. Not bothering to hide her grin, Merewyn focused on repacking her basket.

She glanced once more to the bed, but it appeared her patient was already asleep. Moira was brushing her fingers down Jessie's cheeks in a gesture so heart-wrenchingly sweet, Merewyn felt tears welling.

But then, she *did* tend to be weepier lately.

The love in Moira's expression was clear, and Merewyn knew she cared for Jessie the same she cared for Lara and Brohn, the children she'd birthed. Bairns needed to be protected, whether they were of one's body or not.

Unbidden, Merewyn's fingers dropped to her stomach, gently skimming over the purple gown.

Bairns deserved to be surrounded by love.

Was she being foolish, hoping for that?

Forcing back her tears, Merewyn turned to leave the kitchen... only to find Rocque blocking the way.

Rocque, her lover. *Her man.*

But no' her husband.

He stood, arms crossed, looking every inch the boulder for which he was named. And he looked...*concerned*? Nay, scared, mayhap?

She stepped closer. "She's going to be aright," she whispered, for his ears only.

He blinked, his expression sliding into surprise. "I ken it."

So that hadn't been the cause of his concern?

Her eyes caught on the porridge soaking into his shirt. "Take off yer shirt," she commanded quietly. "I'll wash it for ye so it doesnae set."

With a quick nod, he lifted his arms above his head and made short work of stripping the linen from his torso. *God's Teeth*, but he was a fine-looking man, his muscles stretched like that! She loved the way he shook his head to settle his over-long hair out of his eyes, as his head emerged from the shirt.

Her fingers itched to touch him, and because she *could*, she reached out and spread her palm against the warm skin of his abdomen, reveling in the taut firmness there. She remembered how his skin felt, moving atop her—or under her, or beside her—and her thighs clenched in sudden longing.

Soon.

He was her man, for now at least.

But she'd have to make a decision *soon*.

Because it wasn't fair to keep him waiting.

With a low growl, Rocque pulled her to him, dropping his lips to hers in a hard, quick kiss. It was possessive and full of anger, but Merewyn met it head-on.

It was over far too soon, and did naught but whet her appetite for more.

Soon.

Soon she'd have him...and soon enough after that, she might have naught but her memories of him.

"I'll see ye for supper?" she whispered, her gaze searching his for a sign of what was bothering him.

But he just nodded, jerking his chin down once in a hard acceptance, before he stepped away from her and headed out the door.

Sighing, she clutched his shirt and dropped her hand to her stomach.

She needed to decide, and fast.

Could she marry him? Or would that be dooming her to a lifetime of heartbreak?

And would that be worse than living without Rocque?

CHAPTER 3

"THE WAY he was carrying on, ye would've thought he'd lost a leg!"

Rocque's attention was on the stew in front of him, but he nodded distractedly. "I heard him screaming up at the keep."

"Och, well, the poor lad had a splinter, 'tis all."

He glanced across the table to see Merewyn's smile flash, as she speared a chunk of turnip with her knife. It was such a simple pleasure; sharing stories about their days while they ate together. He'd learned to value this time, and the thought of doing it for the rest of their lives gave him a certain sense of satisfaction.

But apparently, *she* didn't want that.

If she had, she would've agreed to marry him.

Still, he didn't want to be the cause of a bad mood between them, so he nodded as if he'd been paying attention all along. "A splinter?"

Shrugging, she swallowed the bite of food. "Granted, 'twas a big splinter. But I told him if he dinnae want splinters in his arse, he shouldnae drag himself around half-naked across the chapel floor!"

"I'll wager Father Stephen was less than impressed."

She grinned. " 'Tis what happens when yer brothers dare ye to do something daft, I suppose."

She'd been an only child, so he knew she was guessing. Rocque had been raised with his twin brother, both treated like drudges and beaten daily. But when he'd discovered his father's family, they'd accepted him without question, and aye, dared him to do more than a few daft things.

So he had to smile.

"Brothers are a blessing *and* a curse, I've discovered."

She planted her elbows on the table and leaned forward, her lovely gray eyes sparkling in the evening light flooding through the open door and windows.

"Tell me about the time Kiergan convinced ye the Devil had possessed yer boots."

Chuckling, he stabbed his knife into a chunk of meat and reached for his ale. "Ye ken it already."

"Aye, but doesnae mean I cannae hear it again." Still smiling, her hand dropped below the edge of the table, and he thought she might've been touching her stomach. "I'd like to ken it well enough to retell it someday."

Rocque *knew* he wasn't as bright as his brothers—definitely not Malcolm, who was always tinkering or inventing something—but he didn't mind. He'd long ago accepted that each of them had been blessed in different ways. Finn and Kiergan were blessed with charm, Dunc with artistic ability, Malcolm and Alistair with brains...while he was blessed with muscle.

And aye, there were times when he'd wished his brothers hadn't been able to trick him so easily, but then he was sure there were times they'd wished he couldn't punch quite so hard, so they were likely even.

He took a long draught of the ale, then settled back in his chair —'twas a bit wobbly, he'd have to fix it soon—and inhaled deeply. The rafters of her little cottage were always strung with drying herbs from her garden and the forest, and made the place smell of—of...

Well, he wasn't certain what the scent had reminded him of before he'd met her, but now it made him think of *home*. This place was more *home* than the keep or the barracks, now, and Merewyn...well, Merewyn was *home* to him as well.

Smiling, he told her the story she wanted to hear. That one led to another, and soon she was giggling, which made him smile.

Aye, this is nice. 'Twould be nicer with some bairns running around too, making life joyful.

But the thought made him sad. If Merewyn was barren, there'd be no bairns.

If Merewyn was barren, he'd never be laird.

Was this cozy life worth that?

They sat at the table long after the meal was finished, but eventually she stood and began to clean up. He finished his ale and joined her, which made her smile shyly.

St. John's kneecaps, but she made him hard when she peeked up at him like that! Like he was—was her *hero* or something!

She was wearing her hair down, since the meal had started, and he loved the way the red curls cascaded around her shoulders. His fingers itched to wrap themselves through them, to tug her closer.

"Do ye have plans for the evening?" she murmured.

And his cock jumped again.

"Nay," he managed, his voice only a bit strangled. "What did ye have in mind? A walk?"

Since the weather had warmed, they often strolled through the village after supper, greeting neighbors and friends alike. In early summer, he'd realized she did it as much for his benefit as hers; the Oliphants had become comfortable with *both* of them in their leadership roles, and were more likely to stop to chat with them.

The warriors knew Rocque, of course, but now not only did they trust him to lead them in battle, but they stopped him to trade jokes and barbs. And their wives offered little gifts and excess food to Merewyn, in payment for healing.

So, nay, he wouldn't mind a stroll through the village, especially if she'd hold onto his arm the way she sometimes did. And if no one was about to visit with, mayhap they could continue their walk into the little grove of trees besides the river, and he could nudge her up against one of the trees and kiss her until she was ready to—

Oh. He glanced at the board which always rested against the wall by the door. Each morning she made a slash mark on it with a piece of chalk, counting days between saints' feast days and the cycle of the moon. There were certain times in the moon's cycle that she didn't like to make love.

But that was aright, because during the last year he'd realized there was plenty they could do to bring each other pleasure without actual penetration.

Like the time a few months ago, when she'd crawled under the table—while he was still eating supper!—and knelt between his legs and sucked him off like a well-practiced whore. They'd both laughed about it after, but he'd remember *that* for a long time to come, he knew.

His lips twitched.

Come. Heh.

Her eyes were downcast when she stepped up to him, her hands behind her back. Was she going to play the innocent, then?

Placing his finger under her chin, he lifted her gaze to his. "A walk?" he murmured in offer.

"Actually, I was hoping ye would allow me to trim yer hair."

One of his brows flicked upward in surprise. She'd cut his hair just before Hogmany, as he recalled, and it had been the first time in years anyone had cared what his *hair* looked like. But if it mattered to her...

He shrugged. "Aye, have at it."

Which is how he found himself sitting in the wobbly chair—he *really* needed to fix that—out in front of the door to her little cottage. The sun was setting, but there was still more light out there than inside.

She stepped up between his legs, nudging his knees aside so she could reach him, and dragged a comb through his hair.

With her valuable spring shears—Duncan had fixed them for her only a few months ago—she lifted the hair with the comb and trimmed the excess. He couldn't care less what she did to his hair, but wasn't going to pass up the opportunity to touch her.

With her so intent on his head, he placed his large hands on her hips and tugged her closer. She didn't glance down, but her lips curled into a smile as she concentrated on her task. From this angle, he could see the curve of her neck and jaw at his eye level, and he resisted the urge to lean forward and plant a kiss there, knowing she'd just tug him back into position.

So he stayed still, his fingers the only thing he moved, lightly caressing and massaging at her hips and waist.

Was it his imagination, or did she squirm slightly under his touch?

He barely paid any attention to the little pieces of hair floating down around his shoulders, but soon enough she made a satisfied sound and tucked her comb and shears back into the pouch at her hip.

Thinking they were done, he shifted to stand, but froze when her hands went back to his head. And then when her fingers dug into this scalp, he moaned in pleasure.

Kneading and pulling, she massaged the tension from his scalp, then moved to his neck.

If he died and went to Heaven that very night, he was certain it would feel a bit like this.

As he exhaled, he felt the stress of the day—the worry about Da's words, and wee Jessie, and that little shite Hamish—flowed away under her fingers. It felt so damnably good, he almost didn't notice when she tugged his head closer to rest against her bosom.

Almost.

But then, he *would* have to be dead not to notice his own mouth that close to her tits.

By St. John's heart, he could cherish this woman!

His hold on her hips tightened, and her massage traveled down his neck to his upper back and shoulders. He couldn't seem to stop his own hands from moving, and soon he was kneading, massaging, at her waist, then her back, then her arse.

God Almighty, but her arse felt perfect in his hands!

Under his touch, her breathing had changed.

All he had to do was shift slightly, and his lips were against her nipple, which he could feel puckered under the simple purple gown she wore. He nipped at it gently, and she jerked against him.

Her very *scent* had changed, and he knew what that meant.

"Let us go back inside, love," he murmured hoarsely, praying she'd agree.

"Aye," she gasped, and relief flooded him so quickly he was in very real danger of soiling the inside of his kilt.

In one movement, he stood and swept her up and over his shoulder.

She screeched, which turned into a giggle, and then she was slapping at his back.

"Put me down, ye big ox!" she shrieked, her legs kicking uselessly before him as he kicked the door closed.

There were benefits to being so much larger than her.

"Ye like it, dinnae lie," he growled as he smacked her arse.

And her giggles turned to a moan.

In four long strides he was across the cottage, ducking behind the screen which separated her bed from the rest of the room. The bed was his favorite part of the cottage, being large enough to accommodate his bulk. When she slept alone, she barely made a dent in the mattress, but it fit them both perfectly.

Slowly, he tugged her forward, until she was sliding down his chest. One of her legs hooked around his hip on the way down, and he caught the rest of her weight before she touched the ground. In this position, his throbbing cock was pressed *right* where it wanted to be.

"Lass?" he growled in question, not even sure what he was asking, but knowing if he didn't get the answer he needed, he might fall over.

She whimpered, her breaths coming faster and faster, her fingers playing with the hair at the base of his neck. "Please, Rocque."

'Twas all she had to say. Wordlessly, he set her away from him, then spun her around and began to work on the ties to her gown, the ones under her arm. Luckily, he knew this dress.

He knew *everything* about her.

She was his partner in every way that mattered.

In moments, her gown was gaping open and he snaked his hands around her torso to cup her tits, his large, callused thumbs coming to rest on her pert nipples. His lips dropped to her neck, and her hands reached behind her, blindly reaching for his hips as he squeezed her breasts the way she liked.

She moaned again and thrust herself backwards, plastering her arse against his throbbing erection. "God's Teeth, Rocque, ye make me hot!"

"Then climb in the bed, lass, and I'll make ye scream my name."

He knew she liked it when he played the part of the brute, so he slapped her arse for good measure. She turned wide-eyed innocence his way and dragged one forefinger along her lower lip, temptingly.

"Aye, milord," she breathed cheekily, and he grinned in response.

They both made short work of their clothing, tumbling onto the bed in moments. Knowing her preferences, he pulled down the coverlet, so they were lying on the soft linen sheets, and he pulled her across his chest, the back of his hand cupping her head.

But *she* was the one who slammed her lips down atop his, and he caught her moan against his tongue. One of his hands was on her arse, kneading it, and she gyrated against his hip as she reached down to close her fingers around his aching cock.

St. John's dimples, but the lass knew how to make him beg!

The feel of her small hand tugging at his hardness would've been enough to make any man weep, but then she threw a leg across his thigh, and her damp arousal made him growl in need.

This could've been fast and hot, but he'd been thinking about her since that kiss they'd shared in his father's chambers earlier that day, and he refused to be rushed.

Sitting up, he spilled her into his lap. "I'm not done with ye yet," he growled, and her eyes widened in breathless anticipation.

With one quick movement, he had her pressed against the pillows, her legs spread and him kneeling between them. *St. John's tits!* Her cunny was pink and dripping, and 'twas all his.

Letting out a noise somewhere between a groan and a plea, he lowered his lips to the source of her pleasure, and she echoed it.

He dragged his tongue through her weeping slit, and when she bucked against his mouth, he anchored her with one large hand.

"Oh, God, *Rocque!*"

She arched again, and he allowed it, grinning a bit to know how crazy he was making her. He pulled his mouth away from her center long enough to glance up at her. She was cupping her own tits, squeezing them, tugging them together, and her head was thrown back in ecstasy.

I did that to her.

After a year, he knew her body, knew her moods, knew her likes and dislikes.

He knew he could drive her mad by closing his lips around the pearl of her pleasure—*like this*. She moaned again, proving him right. And he knew she loved it when he reached around and cupped her arse.

Sure enough, her thighs fell open even more, welcoming his touch. But she didn't *have* to admit it, not to him.

Because she was his woman, and he knew her.

"Rocque, *please*," she whimpered.

And he rose on his knees, the fingers which had just been probing her wetness now wrapped around his aching cock. He tugged it once, twice, waiting for her to make eye contact.

When she did, he lowered his chin. "I havenae been paying attention to the date, lass."

He was asking if she was comfortable with penetration, and she understood.

Blowing out a breath, she scooched down farther in the bed, simultaneously opening her legs and reaching for him. "It matters naught anymore, I need ye inside me, love!"

Yer bidding is my command, milady.

When he pressed into her, they both let out a sound of triumph. Then her legs were wrapped around his hips, lifting her arse off the bed, and he planted his palms on either side of her head, and they both gave over to the sensations.

Her sheath was as wet and tight as ever—and he was no small man

—but there was something *different* today. Her taste was different, too, he'd noticed, but it was only enough to drive him mad.

She was *his*, and he knew her.

His strokes turned into thrusts, and each time he slammed home, she made that same erotic, desperate noise he'd fallen in love with last year. By all the saints in Heaven, she was glorious!

Mine! Mine! his blood seemed to chant in time to his pounding. *Mine!*

And she squeezed her own tits, moaning as she tightened her leghold on his hips, arching off the bed to meet his thrusts.

Mine!

As the familiar tingling began at the base of his cock, he shifted his weight to one hand and cupped her arse, pulling her against him, his fingers questing beneath her to touch her wetness.

"*Rocque!*" she cried, and began to clench around his cock.

'Twas all he needed. Roaring her name, he slammed into her once more, and as she came around him, he spilled his seed against her womb.

Panting, he fell beside her on the bed, knowing she preferred her space after she found release. Sure enough, her arms fell to her side, one hand brushing his, and he took it. When he looked her way, she was grinning, wide-eyed at him.

"That was incredible, as always."

His grin was slower, but he always took longer to recover than she did.

Bouncing out of bed, she returned with a wet cloth, which she used first to clean him, then herself, before tossing it to the floor and climbing back in beside him. Apparently, the post-coital glow had faded, because she was willing to snuggle up against him.

"Are ye recovered yet, Rocque?"

It took a moment for him to understand her question, then he chuckled. "Insatiable vixen."

"Vixen?" She hummed and turned to press her cheek against his chest. "Did ye just call me a fox?"

"Aye," he drawled, dragging his fingers lazily through her red curls. "Seems to fit."

"Because I'm crafty, sly and beautiful?"

He shook his head, his tone serious when he corrected her. "Because ye're a redhead with cute ears, and I like to see ye down on all fours."

She burst into laughter and sat up, smacking his chest. "Ye ken the way to woo a woman, Rocque Oliphant!"

"I'm trying." He grabbed her hand and, propping his other hand behind his head, pulled her fingers to his lips for a kiss. "I'm half-French, ye ken. Frenchmen are known for their wooing skills."

"Wooing? I'm wooable?"

"We're mid-woo, can ye no' tell?"

"I thought we were post-coital?" She lifted a brow.

Hiding his grin, he nodded. "Post-coital, mid-woo. I'm wooing ye. Consider yerself wooed."

That did it; she burst into giggles again and spread her free hand against his chest, leaning her weight on his torso and tucking her feet under her.

But she only said, "Ye never told me yer mother was French."

He shrugged, careful not to dislodge her. "She was an Oliphant, but always told me she named me Rocque because it sounded French."

Merewyn peered at him, clearly trying to determine if he was teasing her. "I thought 'twas for the size of yer shoulders."

"Och, nay. Malcolm says my shoulders only grew this wide to live up to my name."

Her grin flashed. "Well, I like the thought of yer name being French, and ye being good at wooing."

With a growl, he tugged her closer, dropping her hand to his cheek so he could curl his fingers around the back of her neck. "What do ye think I've been doing all along, lass?"

"Wooing me?" she breathed impishly.

"Would that I could woo ye, but I fear ye're un-wooable."

She was grinning when she dropped a kiss against the corner of his mouth. She didn't pull away.

"What makes ye think I'm un-wooable?" she whispered saucily, and he could tell from her tone what she was thinking.

His other hand came out from behind his head and he reached around to spread his fingers across her lower back. When Merewyn sounded like *that*, he'd best "recover" faster.

Sometimes the lass *was* insatiable.

" 'Tis fairly clear ye want nae part in my wooing, lass."

She wriggled against him. "I love yer wooing. Verra, *verra* much. I would be wooed by ye all day, if I could. I'd be wooed here, across the table over there..." She stretched, slowly straightening her legs until she was lying half across him, one leg thrown across his. "I'd be wooed against that tree in the forest again. Or in the loch where anyone could see. God's Teeth, but *that* was some fine wooing, remember?"

It was half her touch, half the memory of those passionate encounters, which had his cock stirring again.

Fully recovered, aye.

But he was thinking of her claim, as he pulled her in for another kiss.

I love yer wooing.

"Marry me, lass," he whispered against her lips. "Become my woman, in the eyes of God and the clan. I'll woo ye as long and as hard as ye want, then, and nae one will say aught."

"No one says aught now," she said over-loud, using her hand against his chest to push herself upright.

Away from him.

"Lass..."

"Has anyone said aught to ye?" she demanded.

And he had to wince.

They were both respected members of the clan—he the Oliphant commander, her their healer. And if he were honest, he admired her independence, her unwillingness to shackle herself in marriage just for respectability.

But that didn't help when he so desperately wanted to call her *his*.

"Nay," he finally admitted, and knew none of the clan would say aught in front of *him* about her respectability. "But if ye go much longer without a husband—"

"The clan will still appreciate me for my healing abilities," she snapped.

Why was she being so stubborn?

What was wrong with him?

Why was he good enough to sleep with, good enough to share a home with...but not good enough to marry?

"Merewyn, things would be easier if ye agreed to marry me."

"Aye, I daresay they would be."

He was surprised by her agreement, until he heard the sorrow in her tone.

Then she blinked, and her smile seemed just a bit too brittle.

"Now it's my turn!" she chirped, pulling herself up onto her knees and pressing one palm against his chest to hold him down when he made to rise.

"Yer turn for what?"

One of her soft hands dragged down his thigh, and his cock jumped in response. And when she glanced his way, a mischievous twinkle in her gray eyes, he felt himself harden.

"To woo *ye*."

Then she was leaning forward, and his hand went to the back of her head. As her warm mouth closed around his suddenly firm cock, he quit thinking about anything at all.

And let *her* woo *him*.

CHAPTER 4

THE POUNDING at the door woke Merewyn, but that was naught unusual. She was used to being woken in the middle of the night by frantic patients, and she was used to fumbling around in the dark as she got dressed and found her medical supplies.

Of course, she was *less* used to having to untangle herself from a man's arms, but luckily, Rocque had never minded that she liked to *spread out* while sleeping; he never kept her too wrapped up or confined.

Just another example of how well they suited.

As if the three times they'd made love before falling asleep hadn't been enough of a clue.

Nay, no' making love. We were fooking.

He didn't love her.

As she suspected, young Megan's husband was the one pounding on the door, looking terrified. "She sent me to tell ye her water's broken, Healer, and ye're to come at once!"

"Aye, let us go," she said softly, herding the poor man down the street. 'Twas Megan's first bairn, and would likely not come for hours yet, but she'd promised to be there for her patients, and she would be.

Besides, 'twould be a convenient excuse to avoid Rocque's question.

The birth went well, although it took all day. She fell into an exhausted sleep that evening, which meant she avoided having to explain herself to Rocque again. The following night *he* was out late, and he did naught but pull her into his arms when he returned, and fall asleep with his lips pressed against her shoulder.

It was nice. Nicer than she had a right to hope for.

Things would be easier if ye agreed to marry me.

Rocque's words echoed through Merewyn's mind days later. She'd been unable to stop repeating them, alternating between getting mad at the speaker, and mad at herself.

Aye, things *would* be easier if she were to marry him! The clan already considered them a couple; all save those who looked down their noses at her for living with a man not her husband.

But she didn't *have* to marry him. Things would be easier, aye, but not necessary. She'd lived on her own before she'd caught his eye, and she could do it again. Her healing skills were worth meat and bread and enough food to keep her fed. She could trade for anything she couldn't make.

She could live alone again.

But she wouldn't *be* alone, would she?

"*Now* can I get out of bed?" Jessie's tone sounded exasperated, and jerked Merewyn's attention back to the gentle examination she'd been doing on the lassie's recent burns.

The Healer straightened, blinking in surprise.

"Aye, of course." She patted Jessie's arm. "Ye've been lying abed all this time? Remember I told ye the day after the accident that ye could be up and about, as long as the pain wasnae too great."

Jessie didn't reply, but glared mulishly over Merewyn's shoulder.

Merewyn was sitting on the edge of Cook's bed, where she'd been examining the girl. She'd assumed Jessie had just laid down for her exam, but had she really been here the whole time...? Merewyn twisted to see what the girl was frowning at, and saw Moira hurrying into the room.

"Ye've been up and about plenty, lassie," the housekeeper clucked as she reached around Merewyn to squeeze Jessie's hand. "Just because I make ye rest sometimes..."

Jessie huffed, staring up at the ceiling, but Merewyn saw her squeeze Moira's hand in return.

Moira chuckled softly, released the lassie's hand, and slipped from the room.

Merewyn was surprised at the tears which had gathered in her eyes from the sweet display of affection, and hid them by blinking rapidly as she pushed her supplies back into her basket.

'Tis only hormonal.

As Jessie sat up, the healer cleared her throat.

"Moira really cares for ye, ye ken," she said when she felt she could speak without betraying her weepiness. " 'Tis the only reason she has no' let ye resume yer duties."

"Aye," Jessie sighed as she crossed her legs up under her and stared down at her hands in her lap. "I dinnae remember my mam. Moira... she seems like she'd be a nice mam."

Lips tugging upward in a sad sort of smile, Merewyn reached over and took Jessie's hand. " 'Tis no' disloyal to yer family to find comfort and love in yer new station, lassie. I ken ye miss yer father, and Moira's affection will no' replace him...but ye can still be happy here."

The lassie peeked up from under the bonnet she'd started wearing to hide her cropped hair. "I dinnae...I mean, I *like* it here. Everyone is kind to me, and I care for Moira and her family and Cook and Minnie and the others. And I am no' afraid of hard work. Serving meals and cleaning the great hall is no' so hard, really."

Merewyn squeezed her hand. "Well then, it seems to me that life is no' so bad, eh? These burns are naught to be worried about, and ye will heal and grow and 'twill become part of yer past." The lassie would likely always bear the scars from her croft burning, but the porridge burns were barely visible even now.

To her surprise though, Jessie didn't seem reassured by her words. Instead, the girl glanced back down at their joined hands.

"There are some people who are no' kind to me," she whispered.

And Merewyn didn't have to ask who it was. "Has Hamish seen ye since the—the *accident?*"

Jessie shook her head silently.

Hamish had claimed it had been an accident, and Merewyn wouldn't condemn the man without having seen it happen. But she knew that he excelled at using words to hurt or manipulate others. So if it hadn't been an accident, what had prompted it?

"Jessie, has...did Hamish speak to ye *before* the incident?" Had something happened which had precipitated it?

This time, Jessie didn't shake her head. She didn't respond at all, but her grip on Merewyn's hand tightened.

The healer blew out a breath. "Look at me, lassie." When Jessie finally did, Merewyn nodded firmly. "Men like Hamish are no' to be taken lightly. Ye cannae believe his words, and ye cannae be alone with him. Aright?"

When Jessie slowly nodded, Merewyn squeezed her hand once, then released her. "He might no' look it, but he's dangerous. Dinnae listen to him."

"I willnae," Jessie whispered, then brushed her fingers across the healing redness on her neck. "Ye really think I'm better enough to go back to work?"

Grinning, Merewyn stood and slung her basket over her arm. "Would it help if I found Moira and told her so? Are ye so desperate to go back to cleaning and serving?"

When the lassie nodded eagerly, Merewyn chuckled and offered her a hand. "Then get up out of that sickbed and find something to chop or scrub! I'll go find Moira!"

She left the girl happily kneading bread at Cook's side, then went to speak with the housekeeper. Moira's affection for Jessie was clear, and the older woman finally agreed—reluctantly—to allow Jessie to go back to her duties.

Grinning softly, Merewyn headed up the stone stairs for Agatha's chambers, intent on examining the old curmudgeon's gouty foot.

Halfway down the hall, Merewyn had to stop and press her palm against the stone wall. The dizziness caught her unawares sometimes these days, but at least she wasnae ill, as Megan had been in the early months of her pregnancy. She squeezed her eyes shut and took a few deep breaths, and when she opened them, she was able to continue, albeit slower.

By the time she reached Agatha's chambers, she was fine, and she opened the door to find the older woman glowering at her from a chair, her lower leg wrapped and resting on a cushion.

"There ye are, lass! What took ye so long? I've been waiting *forever*."

Grinning, Merewyn pushed the door shut behind her, and crossed to her patient, settling on her knees beside the cushioned stool. "Oh really? Did ye have someplace *else* ye needed to be?"

Agatha tsked loudly. "Dinnae be impertinent. 'Tis unbecoming."

Her hands hovering over the wrapped leg and foot, Merewyn smiled distractedly. "And ye ken I care about becoming *'becoming.'* " Before the old woman could scold her for the silly wordplay, she asked, "Does it feel any better today?"

Agatha Oliphant suffered from occasional bouts of gouts in her left foot, and Merewyn was used to the remedies. When the laird's aunt had sent word she was in pain again, the healer had known what to do.

The old woman blew out a breath. "The cold water was a blessed relief, but Kiergan moaned and complained when I sent him to get it from the loch. Ye'd think I'd asked him to cut off his willy! All I needed was a bowl of cold water—was that too much to ask?"

Merewyn, who was delicately unwrapping the foot, hummed sympathetically. "Young people these days, eh?"

"No respect for their elders."

"Aye, and they use more curse words, too." Merewyn had heard the complaints before. "Not like ye used to when ye were younger, aye?"

"Fook, yes!" Agatha slammed her hand down on the arm of the chair. "And things *cost* more these days, have ye noticed?"

Nodding, Merewyn kept her attention on the wrinkled foot she'd just revealed. "And the winters are colder and longer."

Sighing, Agatha leaned back in her chair. " 'Tis glad I am ye're aware of all the problems plaguing the younger generations, lass."

The healer didn't answer, but carefully lifted Agatha's foot and began to rotate it. Most of the range of movement was there, but she pressed her thumbs against the swelling and began to massage as well as she could.

"Ouch!" Agatha tried to jerk her foot away, but Merewyn held tight. "Are ye trying to kill me lass?"

"I'm rubbing the area, milady. 'Tis all."

The old woman peered suspiciously. "With mystical herbs?"

"Nay, with my thumbs."

Her patient huffed impatiently. "I dinnae ken about all this *modern medicine*. Back in my day, healers had the decency to use scented oils and strange ungulates."

Merewyn hid her smile. "Ungulates are hooved animals, milady."

"What, like horses and camels?"

"If I knew what a camel was, likely."

Agatha sniffed. "And goats? Goats can be mystical creatures, ye ken."

"Aye, goats are ungulates." She moved her thumbs to a different location, and when the old woman didn't complain, kept up her massage. "But 'tis unlikely yer healer used them in any significant way."

"I dinnae ken," muttered her patient. "Ye never met Auld Phebus, my father's healer. The man liked his goats."

Hiding her smile, Merewyn nodded. "Regardless, ye're likely thinking of *unguent*. 'Tis a kind of balm or potion."

The old woman harrumphed, then leaned forward to peer at her foot. "Do ye have any of those thingies?"

Knowing 'twould make her life easier, Merewyn nodded. "Aye. Now close yer eyes so I can apply it."

When Agatha leaned back against her chair, her eyes closed, Merewyn dipped her hands into the cool water—*Have to remember to thank Kiergan for bringing it up*—and muttered under her breath as she placed her hands back on the woman's swollen ankle.

The words were only a rhyme to remember how to distill mandragora, but mayhap they sounded mystical enough for the old woman.

Merewyn worked in silence after that, examining the foot for other signs of gout, and imprinting what it looked like today in her memory, so she could compare tomorrow. She had a tincture mixed from the powdered root of the autumn crocus and musk mallow, and although Agatha would likely complain about the taste, 'twould hopefully reduce the swelling.

"Oh, blast, here he comes again!"

The old woman's muttered remark tugged Merewyn back to the here and now. "What?"

"The drummer, lass." Agatha's eye peeked open. "Do ye no' hear him?"

She must have the ears of a—a— What kind of animal *hears* things really well? A dog? Och, it didn't matter.

But presently, Merewyn heard the muffled drumming, which seemed to seep through the walls of the room. She sat back on her heels.

"Is it…" She squinted at the tapestry hanging along the back wall. "Is it getting closer?"

"Aye," Agatha declared cheerfully as she struggled upright once more. " 'Tis the ghostly drummer of Oliphant Castle! We're doomed!"

"Hurrah," the healer muttered.

The old woman's bony finger jabbed at her shoulder. "And *ye* can hear him! Ye ken what that means?"

Scowling, Merewyn rolled to her feet, rubbing at the spot the finger had poked. "I'm doomed." *Aye, I am.* "I've heard him before."

"Ye have? Ye've heard the drummer?"

Shrugging, the younger woman crossed to a table where a pitcher of water and some flagons sat. "Aye, most evenings I visit the keep, truthfully. 'Tis damned annoying. Although I thought he didnae care to drum in the daytime?"

The drumming was closer now, echoing through the room, and Agatha had to raise her voice to be heard over it.

"Let me get this straight. *Ye*, the village healer, hears the ghostly drummer of Oliphant Castle?"

"Aye?" Merewyn glanced over, the pitcher in hand. "Is that wrong?"

"The ghostly drummer—"

"—of Oliphant Castle, aye," she finished for the old woman. "Doom, aye. Ye said all that. But..." She frowned down at the water in the pitcher. "I havenae heard him the last few times I've visited, now that I think of it."

The drumming was so loud now—was it really coming from *inside* the walls?—she doubted Agatha even heard her last words. But the old woman sniffed anyhow.

" 'Tis because ye're no' *sure* if ye're in love!" she cackled gleefully. "Yer man has heard him, but ye're no' sure!"

In love?

"What?" Merewyn bellowed, over the drumming.

"Hearing the drummer means ye're doomed to fall in love," Agatha screeched. "And Rocque has heard him!"

Him?

"What in damnation are ye—" When she realized the drumming was growing quieter—was the drummer moving on?—Merewyn shook her head and lowered her voice to normal range. "What do ye mean?"

"*Doomed!*" Agatha called happily. "*Doooooooomed!*"

Doomed to fall in love?

Swallowing, Merewyn's hand dropped to her stomach. She knew *her* feelings, but what was Agatha saying about *Rocque's* feelings?

Before she could ask, the door burst open and Nessa—Laird Oliphant's only legitimate child—burst inside. "Have you heard?" she cried, looking torn between tears and hope.

"Aye," snapped Agatha, "The whole bloody keep heard him!"

"I cannae decide if I'm doomed or blessed!" Sniffing melodramatically, Nessa threw herself across her aunt's bed, one forearm covering her eyes.

"Ye heard him, did ye no'? So ye're *dooooomed*, lass!" the old woman cackled. "We all are!"

Merewyn frowned. "If we've all heard the drummer, does that mean *ye're* doomed to fall in love, milady?"

The question had obviously never been asked, judging from the way Agatha jerked upright. She opened her mouth—likely to snap something about *impertinence*—but closed it again. Then she cocked her head to one side and hummed thoughtfully.

"Like that fine-looking man Duncan's wife brought with her from MacIan land?" Merewyn prompted, testing the topic like a questing tongue might probe a loose tooth.

Great analogy.

Thank ye.

"Fergus?" Agatha tapped her finger against her lips, still considering. "Mayhap..."

"What am I to do?" wailed Nessa. "Father's already speaking of *another one!*"

For the first time, Merewyn wondered if mayhap Nessa was speaking of something different. "Milady? *What* have ye heard?"

"Henry Duffus is dead!"

"Oh, Lord help us, no' another one," muttered Agatha.

Nessa pulled herself into a cross-legged position on the bed. "Aye, *another one!* If they're no' already saying I'm doomed, they will after this!"

Wincing, Merewyn focused on pouring water into one of the flagons. This would be Laird Oliphant's only daughter's *fourth* betrothal which ended in the prospective groom's death. All coincidental, of course, but there would be whispers.

"Who's he eyeing this time?" Agatha asked. "Another Henry, no doubt."

Ah, that was right. All the doomed betrothals had been with Henrys, had they not?

"I dinnae ken. I dinnae ask. I've been in my room all morning, trying to think of a way out of this!"

Crossing to the bed, Merewyn handing the young woman the cold water. "Why do ye want a way out of this?"

Glancing up in surprise, Nessa took the water. "Why no'? I dinnae *want* to be married to a man I've never met."

Merewyn shrugged and sank down on the bed beside her. "Ye dinnae want to be married? Or ye dinnae want to be married to a man ye've never met?"

Sniffing, Nessa took a sip of water. "The latter, definitely."

So she'd be fine marrying someone she *had* met? Merewyn exchanged a glance with Agatha.

Interesting.

But the old woman snorted derisively. "Ye're no' one to be giving her advice, Merewyn Oliphant!"

Advice? Rising to her feet, the healer frowned at her patient. "I only asked a question."

"Aye, but all judgey-like." Agatha pointed one bony finger. "*Ye* have been carrying on with a good man for nigh on a year, and despite him all but begging ye to marry him, ye've turned him down each time."

Merewyn's stomach flip-flopped again.

Swallowing, she crossed to the table and reached for the other flagon as she muttered, "I dinnae see how 'tis any of yer business what—"

"Rocque is a good lad."

From her spot on the bed, Nessa spoke up. "He is. Dumb as a rock, of course, but all of my brothers are good men—"

Merewyn whirled. "He is *no'* dumb. He just is no' as quick to speak, as his—yer—brothers."

At Agatha's triumphant grin, Merewyn blew out a breath and shook her head, realizing she'd walked into their trap.

"Aye, he's a good man."

"Then why have ye no' married him?" Nessa asked quietly, cupping the flagon in both hands. "I ken he's asked ye. He told Da, who told Kiergan, who told Lara, who told me."

"Word certainly gets around," Merewyn muttered, picking open the tie on the pouch which held the powdered autumn crocus and musk mallow.

"Well, of course." Nessa sniffed. "Lara *is* my best friend."

As if that excused the rest of the gossip chain.

"Besides, Lara only asked Kiergan because she wanted to know why Rocque has been in such a bad mood lately. I wanted to ask him some questions about defensive techniques using a pike, but didnae want to anger him."

Agatha sniffed. "Why would a gently reared young lady have questions about *pikes*?"

" 'Tis for my latest design!" Nessa put down her water and for the first time since entering the chamber, seemed *pleased* about something. "I want to show the defenders at the walls of Berwick. 'Twas Lara's idea to use onion to get the right color for the threads."

"For what?"

"For the boiling oil, of course!" Nessa grinned. "I cannae wait to start! The looks of terror on the little attackers at the gate will be difficult, but ye ken I love a challenge!"

Her great aunt was shaking her head. " 'Twill be hard to fit it all in, lass."

Nessa froze, her smile growing. She shifted forward, placed her hands on her knees, and winked conspiratorially. " 'Tis what she said!"

Both Merewyn and Agatha reared back at the crude joke. But when they glanced at one another, the older woman's lips were twitching.

Deciding it was on her head to be the voice of reason, Merewyn cleared her throat and tried for nonchalance when she asked, "Where did ye hear that, milady?"

Nessa waved her hand. "Och, 'tis Kiergan's new joke. He says Malcolm invented it, but it takes a clever mind to time it right. *'Tis what she said.* Ye see, it turns the previous comment into a sexual innuendo—"

"I understand it," Merewyn interrupted, not sure she wanted to learn just how much Nessa knew about *sexual innuendos*. But then her shoulders relaxed, and she offered a sheepish grin. " 'Tis a fine joke, I suppose."

But Agatha, her lips pressed tightly together, merely snorted. When the younger women looked at her, her nostrils flared. "Berwick? Burning oil? Ye are a strange lass, to be sure."

Nessa shrugged. "I like embroidery. 'Tis no' strange."

" 'Tisnae the *embroidery* I object to." Shaking her head, Agatha turned to Merewyn, who was finishing stirring the powder into the water. "But I will no' be distracted, Healer. Why have ye said nay to Rocque? Why will ye no' marry him?"

Sighing, Merewyn crossed to hand the old woman the tincture. "Because he does no' love me," she said simply.

Frowning, Agatha sipped at the drink. "Ye think he doesnae love ye? When he has heard the drummer?"

"I've been with the man for nigh a year, milady," Merewyn pointed out, crossing her arms and glaring at her patient to drink the medicine to reduce her swelling. "And living with him for most of that. He's never once mentioned love."

"Men never do," Nessa offered mournfully. "Except Da. He's a good man."

"All yer brothers are," Agatha snapped, then glared up at Merewyn. "Although I'll deny it if ye repeat that."

Merewyn's lips twitched. "Yer secret is safe with me."

"Good." The old lady nodded forcefully, then downed the rest of the tincture with a grimace. "This tastes like snail piss."

Taking the flagon, Merewyn raised a brow. "Ye ken what snail's piss tastes like?"

"I have an imagination, do I no'?" Agatha's voice dropped to a mutter. "Vinegar and slime, is what I imagine."

She wasn't wrong.

"Healer," Nessa prompted quietly.

When Merewyn turned, the young woman was smiling a little sadly. "Rocque *is* a good man. I dinnae ken if he loves ye, but *ye* sound verra certain. Have ye asked him?"

Well...nay.

Her silence must've been all the answer Nessa needed, because she nodded encouragingly. "Ask him," she whispered.

"Aye, ask him!" Agatha's voice cracked like a whip, startling Merewyn. "Ask him if he loves ye, before ye go consigning yerself to a life of misery."

Ask him?

"Ye want me to just…what? Lay my feelings out? Bare my heart?" Merewyn snorted, irritated by how angry she sounded, but not knowing how to stop. "I'll no' allow him that power."

"Aye, 'tis yer problem." Now *Agatha* was the one sounding all judgey. "If ye love someone, ye're willing to grant them power. They hold yer heart."

How do ye ken?

She wanted to snap it, but held her tongue.

Nessa was the one who was the most reasonable. "Merewyn, ye dinnae have to bare yer heart," she said softly. "Especially if ye dinnae ken his answer. But ye owe him an explanation, at least."

Standing there in the fine chambers of Oliphant Castle, Merewyn's fingers curled around the flagon, her knuckles going white.

Ye owe him an explanation.

Aye, she was beginning to suspect she owed him an explanation about a *lot* of things. Could she give him one—at least one—without having to lay out her own feelings? She couldn't bear the thought of him knowing her most intimate feelings, without knowing his.

But *something* had to change, and quickly.

Unbidden, the fingers of her other hand dropped to her waist, to skim across her stomach. New life grew there, and in only a few short months, 'twould be obvious to all who looked at her.

It wouldn't be fair to Rocque if she didn't tell him first.

But she needed to get this *marriage* discussion out of the way.

Could she do it without crushing her own heart?

Glancing up, she met Lady Agatha's serious gaze.

"Tell him what ye're thinking, at least, lass," the old lady prompted.

Merewyn was beginning to suspect she didn't have a choice.

CHAPTER 5

THIS WAS the first evening he'd gotten to spend any time with her in a few days, and it was nice to just walk together.

They'd shared dinner—the bread had been a gift from a grateful mother, and Rocque had brought down the deer whose haunch Merewyn had roasted. Now they were both blissfully full and enjoying the early evening light.

"I love the way the wood smells after a rain, do ye no'?"

Her murmur seemed somehow appropriate for their surroundings.

There *had* been a light rain that afternoon, and the forest was still damp. The earthy scents of loam and decaying leaves mixed with a sort of *freshness*. Little drops still glistened on blades of long grass here and there, and sounds seemed muted.

"Aye, lass." He inhaled deeply. " 'Tis close to Heaven."

She didn't reply, but reached over and took his hand. Their fingers entwined, as if it were the most natural thing in the world, and she stepped off the path, pulling him behind.

Dare he hope they were heading for some privacy?

Under his kilt, his cock twitched.

Down, lad.

Merewyn carried her herb basket. 'Twas likely she was just searching for—ah!

She made a pleased little sound and released his hand to squat at the base of an oak.

"Hyssop," she said, pitching her voice over her shoulder to him. " 'Tis good for purgatives and ridding lungs of phlegm."

"Do ye need help?"

She stood again, dusting her hands against her dress—a serviceable green woolen gown—and offered him a little smile and a shake of her head.

"Nay, 'twas simple."

Then she took his hand again, and ducked under a low-hanging branch.

He was fine letting her take the lead. They were well within Oliphant land, and he knew they were safe here. Besides, he was never without his blade, and he could protect her if there *was* an unseen threat.

But 'twas hard to think of a threat, when the evening was so relaxing. Even the birdsong seemed gentled, and he caught himself smiling softly as she pulled him around a large oak, heading for the sound of a burbling stream.

"Ye ken," he said softly, "I've often imagined taking my son out into this wood on evenings like this."

She shot him a surprised look. "Really? Why the evening?" she teased.

Shrugging, he followed her into a small clearing. "Because I assumed I'd be busy all day with my duties. He'd be at home with his mother."

"What if his mother had duties too?"

Was it his imagination, or had her voice gone a little harder there?

"Ye mean like healing?" Under his beard, his lips twitched, and he moved to stand in front of her, pulling her around to face him. "Then he'd be with someone else. Mayhap Moira could care for him the way she raised my brothers. Or another woman in the village."

He ducked his chin, to make certain he held her gaze as he lowered his voice. "Because his mother's duties would be as important as my own, and I couldnae ask her to give them up to play nursemaid."

Her lips formed an "oh," and his cock jumped again. St. John's kneecaps, she was beautiful! Beautiful and stubborn and headstrong, that was his Merewyn!

She blinked and looked away. Before he could drag her attention back, her little pink tongue darted out across her lower lip, and he tugged her closer. 'Twas like a challenge, when she did that—it made him want to take that lip in between his teeth and *suck*.

"Ye want a son?" she asked in a small voice.

"Son or daughter." He shrugged. "If my daughter wanted to learn to hunt the stag, I could teach her too, I suppose."

"But a son..." She swallowed and peeked up at him. "A son would mean ye'd be laird. Ye'd win yer father's challenge, if ye were the first to give him a grandson, would ye no'?"

He'd never considered that. "He wouldnae—" Rocque stopped, shook his head once to try to get his thoughts in order, then continued. "I mean, there's nae telling if *my* son would be the eldest, aye? And besides... I dinnae ken if I am the best choice for laird."

Her gray gaze had sharpened, and she shifted closer, until her breasts were brushing against his chest. Their fingers were still entwined, and she squeezed.

"Why do ye say that, Rocque?"

"Say what?"

"Why do ye think ye might no' be the best choice for laird, after yer father is gone?"

Oh Hellfire, why was she asking the *hard* questions?

He shrugged again. "I ken I'm no' the smartest of—"

"Ye're perfect."

His teeth snapped shut, stunned by her impassioned defense. And when she lifted her free hand—had she dropped her basket?—to cup his cheek, Rocque's knees went weak.

"You are perfect the way ye are, Rocque Oliphant. I willnae allow *any* person—brothers or nay—say otherwise."

His eyes searched hers, looking for the joke.

All he saw was sincerity.

"Ye really think that?" he whispered.

Her fingernails scratched against his beard. "I *ken* it."

His lips parted on her name—half-sigh, half-plea. "*Merewyn.*"

Pushing herself up on her toes, she pressed her lips to his. And with a groan, he wrapped his free arm around her back, pulling her flush against him.

Ye are perfect.

Being with this woman made him *feel* perfect, made him feel *alive.* Like he could do anything!

Concerns and worries about life just...just slid away when he was with her. When her lips tugged at his like this, when she made those sexy little noises, he knew his life was perfect.

St. John's nostril!

She had him harder than the oak trees surrounding them, and all she'd done was *kiss* him.

With another erotic moan, she untangled her fingers from his and lifted her other hand to the hair at the back of his head, tugging him closer.

Any closer and I'll be inside of her.

Aye, please!

There was a part of his mind which couldn't be shut down, a part which was always on the alert, aware of danger. But the birds were still chirping, the brook still babbling, and she'd just lifted her left leg to wrap around his, pushing her core against the very part of him which longed for it.

Aye, danger could go hang itself.

The hand not holding her desperately to him rose to cup her breast through her gown, and when she moaned against his mouth, he quickly tugged down the neckline to expose her nipple.

The noise she made *then* had him wrenching his lips from hers and dropping them to that nipple, while her fingers tugged at his hair and her panting breaths urged him on.

"*Rocque,*" she mewed softly, her pelvis gyrating desperately.

"Aye, lass," he whispered against her skin, as he switched his attentions to her other tit. "I ken what ye like."

"Ye ken—" She was panting. "*Please!* Make me yers!"

Mine.

He slowly straightened, and met her passion-fogged eyes. Aye, he knew what she liked.

He smiled. In one swift motion, he'd tugged her gown lower down her arms, exposing both breasts to the cool evening air.

She mewled desperately and lowered her hands to them, pushing them together and squeezing her puckered nipples.

Aye, he knew how to make her hot.

Make me yers.

He lifted one hand to her cheek, then twined it through the curls atop her head. He pushed downward.

"Then on yer knees, lass."

BLESSED VIRGIN, *yes!*

Dimly, Merewyn wondered if mayhap she should leave the Christ-child's mother out of things when she was about to suck a man's cock, but there were times she just had to pray.

She *knew* she was a strong woman, and could survive on her own. But when Rocque spoke to her in that commanding voice, she was thankful she was already kneeling, because her thighs clenched so hard, she couldn't have stood.

With one hand still wrapped through her curls, his other lifted his kilt, and with an eager groan, she lunged forward.

His cock was as thick as the rest of him, and she had to drop one of her breasts to reach beneath it and wrap her fingers around its base. God Almighty, but he tasted divine! She loved that he cared enough for cleanliness that she could still smell the soap on him.

She let him know she was ready by inhaling deeply and sinking back on her haunches; he steadied her head as he pushed his thickness past her tongue and into her throat. She'd long ago gotten over the panic which came from not being able to breathe, and instead met his eyes, showing her trust.

Sure enough, he let out a hoarse, *"By all the saints, lass!"* and pulled himself free long before she needed him to, and the flood of saliva was tinted with the taste of his salty sweetness.

She licked at him, and when he dropped his other hand to her head with a groan of surrender, the rush of *power* she felt, holding this man in her mouth, caused a flood of desire between her thighs.

As he used her mouth, she scrambled for her gown, shifting her weight—the friction delightful as her thighs rubbed against one another—to pull her skirts out of the way.

Finally, they were free, and she was able to yank them up and delve her fingers between her legs.

Aye!

She was as wet as she knew she'd be, and when she spread her thighs and dragged her first two fingers through her slit, she shuddered with desire.

The burning—yearning—was building inside her core, and when she lifted her free hand to cup his bollocks, he groaned and pushed against her once more.

"Lass," he choked, "ye're making me crazed."

Good, she wanted to tell him, but her mouth was full of *him*. Instead, she hummed against his cock, and when he groaned in pleasure, did it again.

One of his hands dropped to his own cock, circling the base and holding it steady as he increased his pace, thrusting into her mouth with soft grunts. She squeezed his bollocks, loving the way it made his breath catch, and pressed two fingers up inside her.

She damn near came off the grass, it felt so good. Not *perfect*—nothing would feel as perfect as *him* inside her, but...she curled her fingers, as if beckoning herself toward release, and felt her climax building.

"That's it," he murmured. "That's a good lass. Ye *like* doing this, do ye no'? Ye like touching yerself, while I use yer mouth. Come for me, lass. Come for me like a good girl."

Gasping against his cock, she did.

Her release burst over her, as she curled her fingers inside her cunny and rode the waves of pleasure, rocking against his cock.

But with a roar, he pulled himself from her mouth, jerked once, twice, and climaxed explosively. A thick white stream burst from the tip of his cock and splashed against her neck and chest, spilling down across her breasts.

Breathing heavily, she reached for her nipple and caught one strand of his pleasure as it reached the tip of her breast. She lifted that finger to her mouth as she gently withdrew her fingers from her softly pulsating core.

As she met his eyes—still on her knees—the taste of his salty arousal exploded against her tongue.

"*God in Heaven*," he groaned, and staggered back to press one hand shakily against the strong trunk of an oak. "*God in Heaven!*"

"Aye," she drawled quietly, not sure if it was a prayer or a praise.

Or both.

He was still staring at her, wide-eyed, as she shifted herself to rest on her arse, holding her weight on one palm pressed against the grass. Then he shook himself and cleared his throat.

Her basket was where she'd dropped it—the hyssop had rolled out, but she'd collect it—and he reached for one of the cloths he knew would be in there. She always brought plenty to wrap herbs in, but for now, this one would serve another purpose.

She watched as he dropped to one knee by the stream to soak the cloth, then squeezed out the excess. Before he saw to himself, he returned to her and—while she held herself unmoving—he gently wiped his seed from her neck and chest. It took two trips to the brook, and the whole time she remained still and marveled at his gentle care.

Finally, on one knee before her, he handed her the cloth to clean her hands, then tossed it to one side and pulled her into his arms.

She felt *safe* here.

"St. John bless me, lass," he whispered against her hair. "Ye shouldnae allow me to treat ye so."

Surprised, she jerked away to meet his eyes. "Why no'? Ye ken I like it when ye mark me like that."

'Twas not a lie. Holding him in her mouth made her feel *powerful* in a way she couldn't describe.

And she was a woman who liked being in control.

He tsked softly and moved to sit beside her. Then with a sigh, he leaned back, resting one hand behind his head as he pulled her down atop his chest.

Her lips twitched when she realized he was still wearing his sword. They were both still fully dressed, in fact, now that she'd tucked her breasts back in and re-tied everything.

He was smiling sleepily, although 'twas hard to tell behind that beard. She was invigorated—as she always was after their love-making—and reached up to scratch at his jaw.

" 'Tis time to trim this bush."

"Bah! Ye like it."

Her grin grew. "I like the way it feels against my skin, aye. But I dinnae like the idea of no' being able to see yer face, when it gets this long. I worry about losing ye. Or ye hiding a leg of mutton in here. Or small children."

She expected him to chuckle at her jibe, but the look in his eyes turned a little sad as he shifted his gaze up to the sky peeking through the branches above them. When she glanced upward, she could see the brilliant colors of a summer sunset in the Highlands, and wondered what he was thinking.

Small children.

Was he thinking of their earlier conversation about becoming laird? Or about having children?

Her fingers fluttered to the hollow at the base of his throat, her touch hesitant.

Even now she was carrying his bairn. And she hadn't told him.

He must be told.

Aye, aye, she'd tell him.

Because even if there was no future for them, even if she chose to raise their bairn alone, he would have to be told.

And in that moment, she realized a truth she'd never considered: Rocque *was* a good man, and he'd be a good father. Even if he wasn't her husband, she could trust him to do what was right by the bairn.

Slowly, her lips curled into an amazed grin and she pushed herself up to sit at his side. Her bairn—*their* bairn—could have both a mother and a father, even if they weren't married.

"Why will ye no' marry me, lass?"

Oh, fook.

Just like that, her burgeoning good mood evaporated.

Inhaling deeply, she shifted her gaze back up to the sunset and squared her shoulders.

"Because I am strong. I can live alone. I dinnae *need* a husband," she began.

"I ken it well." One of his large hands rested on the small of her back, the motion comforting. "But ye dinnae *have* to."

"Nay, I dinnae." She swallowed, not sure how to explain, now that it was time. " 'Tis my choice, and that's the point."

She dropped her eyes, only to find him frowning thoughtfully as his gaze caressed her face. Remembering Nessa's words from this afternoon, she struggled to make her tongue work.

Ye owe him an explanation.

It was possible to explain her reasoning without laying bare her heart, wasn't it?

So she tried again. "I can choose to live with a man—to yoke myself to him—if I want, but if I dinnae, I will still survive thanks to my skills and trade with the villagers."

"Is that what you want?" His voice sounded strangled.

"Nay," she confessed quietly. "I want a strong, happy marriage."

"Then why won't you say aye to me, lass?"

"Because you don't love me!" The words burst from her lips before she could stop them, and she clenched her teeth to keep more damning evidence from spilling forth.

But when he slowly sat up, his frown deepening, Merewyn drew her knees to her chest and wrapped her arms around them. His hand dropped away from her back, and she felt more than a little deprived.

"My parents..." She jerked her head, embarrassed by the way her voice wavered. "My mother loved my father. My father loved ale. He was kind enough, but didnae love her the way she loved him." Merewyn was careful to keep her tone steady as she relived those years of pain. "I saw what that did to her—to them both. So much hurt and bitterness in that home." Her voice dropped to a whisper. " 'Twas almost a relief when I lost them."

He rested one elbow against his raised knee, and looked as if he might say something. Before he could, she hurried her explanation, determined to get it said.

"I promised myself long ago I would only marry for love. If I couldnae marry for love, I'd rather live alone." She lifted her chin and met his eyes, challenge in her tone when she added, "I could even raise a child alone, as long as I knew I had my pride."

His brows dipped in, and she knew he was considering her words. He always looked like that when he was thinking.

Finally, he exhaled. "Ye willnae marry me...because ye dinnae love me?"

Was it her imagination, or did he sound...*hurt?*

She swallowed.

This was it.

This was the moment to confess her feelings.

The moment to tell him how she'd fallen in love with him months and months ago. How she'd accepted him as her lover because of his strength and humor and smile, but had let him into her heart because of how he *acted*. Who he *was*.

She'd fallen in love with his concern, his gentleness, the way he could make her burn with just one look. The way he took care of her needs and wanted to make her happy.

Aye, she loved him. She could happily spend her life with such a man.

But she couldn't—*wouldn't*—allow herself to spend her life with a man who didn't love her in return. She'd seen what that had done to her mother, and she had more pride than that.

Much more pride.

Too much pride to tell him how she felt, if he was unwilling to bare his own heart.

Sadly, she shook her head. Inhaling deeply, she met his eyes.

"Nay, Rocque. I willnae marry ye because *ye* dinnae love *me.*"

His eyes rounded, and she could see the disbelief in their lovely blue depths. Disbelief? She nodded, her jaw tensing, willing him to understand what she was saying.

"Love ye?" he repeated in a strangled whisper.

'Twas not a declaration. 'Twas not a denial.

As far as Merewyn was concerned, he'd just confirmed everything she believed.

Suddenly feeling drained, she pushed herself to her feet, staggering slightly as blood rushed to her head. He didn't reach for her, and once she was steady, she turned to scoop up her basket and the fallen hyssop.

When she turned back to him, he hadn't moved. Nay, he was still sitting here on the grass, one arm draped across his raised knee, looking…well, she couldn't read his expression. That was the problem with that beard. It made him all—all—all *blurry.*

Blurry?

Nay, that wasn't because of his beard. She lifted one set of fingertips to her cheek to catch the tear as it spilled from her eye.

I love ye!

She wanted to shout it, to beg him to love her in return.

But she wouldn't. *Couldn't.*

Forcing her shoulder straight, she turned in the direction of the village. But at the edge of the small clearing, she paused, and debated with herself.

Finally, deciding there was *no way* she'd be able to maintain her pride if she turned to look at him, she lifted her chin and, staring straight ahead, whispered, "Goodbye, Rocque."

Then she darted among the trees, half-hoping, half-dreading he'd come after her.

He didn't.

CHAPTER 6

YE DINNAE LOVE ME.

She'd been so *certain* when she'd said it, that's what was really galling.

Rocque's fist slammed into the stuffed bag, sending it swinging on a short arc. When it returned, he jabbed the thing twice more, releasing some of his frustration one little burst at a time.

St. John's sacred hairline, why had she sounded so *certain*?

Growling, he punched the bag again, then pivoted as it swung, and lashed out sideways with a booted foot, catching on the return.

It felt *good* to hit something. 'Twas what he'd always done, when he was uncertain of his life. Hitting things always helped him release anger and frustration, and he thought more clearly when he was sweating.

His fists jabbed out once, twice, thrice, striking the bag at various points, causing the entire tree limb to shudder. Soon, he was panting in exertion, which was always his goal.

He'd always been this way, although he hadn't grown into his muscles until Da had started working him. But growing up, he *had* been taller than most other boys, and none would spar with him. So his mother had sewn him a bag, which she'd stuffed with sheep's wool, the discardings her uncle allowed her to keep, and hung it up for him to hit. 'Twas a simple design, but had saved many heads over the years.

Of course, if Rocque had known how to really *hit* back then, instead of merely *taking* punches, mayhap his mother would still be alive. He slammed his fist into the bag again. Mayhap he could've taken her and Malcolm away from that living hell and returned to Oliphant land much sooner.

The growl which escaped his lips was unexpected, but nothing new. When the bag swung back, he jerked his elbow into the leather and followed it with a kick. The guilt of his mother's death had hung over him for years, despite knowing it wasn't his fault. He was *used* to these feelings.

It was *Merewyn* who had him all tied in knots now.

Breathing heavily, he stepped back, but kept his fists up, as if the bag might attack him.

St. John's tits! She'd told him she couldn't marry him because *he didn't love her*!

And as much as he wanted to spit at the sentiment, he couldn't deny what he saw around him every day. Finn loved Fiona, and had since last autumn; that didn't make him less of a man.

Duncan was the least demonstrative person Rocque knew, but *he* was certain of his love for Skye.

And even Da still mourned his lost love, the lady whose death had sent him into the village to seek comfort in Mam's arms, a lass barely into womanhood. He'd regretted her family's treatment of Mam, of course, when he'd found out...but he'd never cared for her the way he'd cared for his lady love.

Love *was* possible. And he respected Merewyn enough to consider her words. She'd finally told him her reasoning for declining his proposal, and what irritated him was that he'd *understood* what she was saying.

Not wanting to marry someone because they didn't love you... well, that made sense.

With a muttered curse, he stepped up to the bag again, and wrapped an arm around the upper part. Holding it still, he slammed his right fist into the leather, feeling the reverberations through the bag and into his shoulder.

Her words echoed in his mind with each punch.

Ye.

Dinnae.

Love.

Me.

Grunting, he jerked his knee up, hard, where an opponent's stomach would be if the bag were a man.

But it wasn't; it was a reinforced leather bag stuffed near to bursting with wool, then sewn shut. Heavy rocks lined the bottom to keep it from swinging too wide, and it was one of these his knee slammed into.

"*Fook me!*"

He released the bag and staggered back, keeping the weight off his throbbing knee.

"Shite," he muttered, limping backward and shaking out his arms and hands while glaring at the bag. "*Shite.*"

"Did that thing finally get the best of ye?"

The drawled question had him whirling and crouching, bringing his fists up into a protective stance even as he recognized the voice. Malcolm's easy smile was welcome, even as his twin pushed away from the tree where he'd been leaning.

With his arms crossed and one booted foot in front of the other, he looked the picture of ease. But Rocque could see the concern in his brother's blue eyes, so he forced himself to straighten and release some of the tension he was holding.

But he couldn't hold in the wince as he shifted his weight to both knees.

Malcolm's smile eased. "Are ye hurt?"

"Nay." Rocque's voice sounded hoarse to his own ears. "I'll be aright."

Swallowing, he turned back to the bag and exhaled. "Why are ye here?"

"Because ye've been avoiding us all day, and ye looked like ye needed to talk."

Avoiding us. Mal was right. He *had* been avoiding his family, other than the training he'd done with the men that morning, and even that hadn't been enough to distract him from his thoughts.

With a growl, his fist jabbed into the bag, and he followed it with another from the opposite fist. The bag swung out, and he caught it on its return with another volley.

One, two, *swing.* One, two, *swing.*

The rhythm was comforting.

He hadn't gone home last night.

Home? Scoffing at himself, he jabbed at the bag again. *Home* was Merewyn's cottage. He hadn't gone back to Merewyn's cottage last night. Well, he hadn't gone *in.*

He'd laid there on the forest floor, thinking about her words, long after she'd left. Finally, worry for her roused him, and he trooped back to her cottage, only to find the candles dark. He'd stood there in her garden for longer than he wanted to admit, staring at the door and wondering if she wanted him to join her, before finding his bed in the barracks.

And he'd been avoiding *everyone* since then.

This time, when he slammed his fist into the bag, his breath escaped with a grunt.

And suddenly, Malcolm was there, catching the bag on its swing, and holding it.

Rocque was breathing heavily, his hair sticking to his neck with sweat, and still he stood there, fists up, waiting for his brother to release his toy.

"Let it go," he growled.

"Nay," Mal said simply. "The rope is fraying from the parabolic motion. I'll have to replace it for ye soon."

Surprised, Rocque's eyes flicked upward, and sure enough, the loops holding the thing to the tree limb *were* fraying. Sighing, he stepped back.

"Can ye add more heft to the thing so it doesnae swing so hard?"

His twin smirked. "Ye mean more rocks, Rocque? Can yer knees handle that?"

His knee *hadn't* ached, until just that moment. Scowling, Rocque limped over to a boulder and sank down upon it, one hand rubbing at his bruised joint.

"I dinnae care *how* ye do it," he muttered. "Just make it heavier. The one Mam made me didnae swing so far."

Mal's smile seemed a little sad as he released the bag and gently halted its swing. Without looking up, he said softly, "I designed that one, too, ye ken."

Nay, he *hadn't* known that. Rocque's gaze jerked up. "Ye did?" They'd been mere lads then.

But Malcolm nodded, still staring at the leather as his hands swept across the seam. "She was so worried for ye. Ye carried so much anger, especially toward Uncle. Mam was afraid ye would lash out at him again, and she wouldnae be able to protect ye." He looked up and met Rocque's eyes. "So I invented the bag. Something for ye to hit, instead of *someone*."

Rocque swallowed, remembering what he used to be like in those days.

"So when we came here, 'twas easy enough for ye to build me another one?"

His twin shrugged. "Well, by then Moira did the actual sewing. And stuffing." He patted the seam. "The more wool crammed in here, the more blows it can take. *This* one has double-layered leather too, which is ideal. It can withstand *all* yer anger."

Blowing out a breath, Rocque dropped his gaze to his palms. All his anger? Mayhap. The bag had stood up well enough so far.

But he was a different man than he'd been in his youth. He'd carried so much anger at the injustices in the world. It had been Da— and Moira, and his brothers—who'd taught him how to channel that anger, how to control it. He'd become a leader, thanks to their influence, and punching Hamish in the nose the other day had been the first time he'd hit another man in anger in a very long time.

'Twas worth it.

One corner of his lips twitched wryly. Aye, he might've been born illegitimate, but Hamish was the real bastard.

"So…" Malcolm's voice was closer, but Rocque didn't look up from his study of his palms. "What are ye angry about now?"

"I'm no' angry." His hands curled into fists, and he forced them to loosen. "I'm frustrated."

His twin hummed, and settled himself on the ground beside the boulder. Close enough to touch, but not.

Malcolm had always been like this boulder; steady, certain. There when he needed someone who understood him.

Rocque might've been named for the stone upon which he sat, but 'twas Malcolm who'd always been his rock.

His brother pulled one knee up and rested his arm across it. His hair was the same russet waves as Rocque, but *he* looked as if he kept it trimmed neatly…without Merewyn to remind him. Rocque blew out another frustrated breath at the thought of how she'd taken care of him, and wanted to pat his brother's shoulder the way they'd done as children.

He didn't.

"Frustrated, then." Mal shrugged, without looking up at him. He sounded merely curious, but Rocque knew he'd sit here all day until he learned what he needed to know. "What has ye so frustrated?"

Inspiration struck.

Rocque cleared his throat. "What do ye ken about—about how babies are made?"

Mal jerked as if he'd been hit, and slowly turned to stare incredulously up at Rocque. His mouth had gone slack, and his blue eyes were wide with shock.

"Ye want—" He shook his head. "Ye're asking me how *sex* works?"

"Bah!" Rocque slapped him on the shoulder as he straightened. "I ken the *mechanics* of it verra well. 'Twas *bairns* I'm asking about."

Mal's eyes narrowed. "Why?"

'Twas difficult to say such things to another man while looking him in the eye, so Rocque shrugged and leaned forward, propping his elbows on his knees and staring down at his laced fingers.

"Merewyn hasnae— In the last year, she's no'..." He swallowed. "Da was the one who suggested she might be..."

St. John's big toe! He couldn't say it.

But his brother hummed thoughtfully, and from the corner of his eye, Rocque saw him settled back into his spot, his gaze across the clearing.

"She has no' fallen pregnant, and ye think she might be barren?"

Rocque swallowed. It took him two tries to croak "Aye."

"Let me ask ye this, brother: How much would it matter? If Merewyn *is* barren."

I want bairns.

Until Da's declaration, Rocque hadn't really considered a future as a father. But he'd been thinking of it more often these days, and knew he wanted to raise sons and daughters to follow after him.

But all he said was, "If I want to become laird, I need a son."

The little noise Malcolm made sounded almost...disappointed? As if Rocque had answered incorrectly.

"Aye, ye do. Ye'd made a fine laird, if 'tis what ye want. And Merewyn will make a fine wife. So I'll ask again: If she's barren, how much would that matter to ye?"

Rocque got the impression his brother was holding his breath, same as he was. Neither spoke, neither looked at one another.

Because Rocque wasn't sure *how* to answer.

If Merewyn was barren, and he married her, he wouldn't be able to become laird.

But he'd have Merewyn as a wife, and they could always adopt children. There were plenty of bairns, others like Jessie, who needed homes.

He squeezed his fingers tighter, the knuckles whitening against one another, and tried to ignore the pain in his stomach.

How important *was* the lairdship, anyhow?

Could he give it up, if it meant keeping Merewyn?

And the moment he posed the question to himself like that, he knew the answer.

Aye.

Aye, having Merewyn as his wife would be worth giving up a chance at becoming Laird Oliphant.

Besides, what was lairdship except more headache?

Of course, all of this was moot if he couldn't convince her to marry him.

Before he could figure out a way to explain this all to Malcolm, is brother blew out a breath and reached for a nearby stick. "Look, there are plenty of reasons Merewyn hasnae gotten pregnant, and they have naught to do with yer prowess or penis, aye?"

Rocque's head jerked upright. "What?"

"Assuming ye've been spilling inside her, and please dinnae confirm nor deny that, because I dinnae need to ken *everything*, then there are other explanations. She's a midwife, surely she kens of teas to drink to keep herself without child."

"But..." Rocque blinked. "The Church says—"

The look his brother shot him was part exasperation and part disbelief. "I ken what the Church says far better than ye, brother, remember?" Malcolm had once thought to take holy orders, if only to have access to the Abbey's library. "But clearly women are doing *something*, or we'd be overrun with bairns, based on the number of times men cannae control their urges."

Rocque frowned. He'd never seen Merewyn drinking tea... "What are the other explanations?"

"Mayhap she's just good at counting."

Counting?

"Counting what?" he repeated.

"Days." Malcolm used the stick to make seven ticks on the ground, then seven more. He jabbed the end into the dirt at the beginning, and dragged it through to the fourteenth mark. "A fortnight after her menses begins, a woman is at her most fertile. If Merewyn—or any woman—is clever and good at counting, she can reasonably prevent pregnancy by declining sexual intercourse during that time."

Slowly straightening, Rocque thought of the board with the marks Merewyn hung on the wall. The phases of the moons were there, and he knew she used those. There were times of the moon's cycle she either turned him down completely, or requested he not enter her. He'd always thought that was because she enjoyed the feel of his tongue—and his beard against her inner thighs—just as well.

But was she—had she been *counting*?

With a whispered curse, Rocque scrubbed a hand over his face. "I'm nae good at maths," he muttered.

"Aye, I ken it."

But rather than making him feel ignorant, Malcolm shifted forward so he could rub out his marks with one palm, and smoothed the dirt. "Look here." He drew an odd-shaped squiggle. "This is a woman's womb. It is connected here to her heart, and here to her sheath. She uses a man's seed to make a bairn, aye?"

He planted the end of the stick in the middle of the womb-squiggle while Rocque squinted down at the sketch.

From this angle the "womb" looked a little like a nut. Mayhap a bean. He twisted his head. From overhead, a squirrel chittered at him, and he wondered if the damned thing was wondering why two grown men were sketching *beans* in the dirt.

If *anyone*—even another one of their brothers—walked into this clearing right now, to find the two of them peering at a drawing of a woman's *inner workings*, Rocque would—he would—well, he wasn't sure what he'd do. Was it possible to die of embarrassment?

Embarrassment caused by finding out how babies were made?

He lowered his voice, just in case any brothers or clansmen or *squirrels* were listening in. "I suppose that makes sense."

"Once a month, her body prepares for the bairn, but if she's not taken seed when she's most fertile, then her body doesnae create a babe." He swished the stick back and forth in the dirt in a way which made Rocque want to press his knees together to protect his dangly bits. "And instead bleeds."

"She bleeds because she's no' pregnant?"

Malcolm turned to flash him another vaguely amused grin. "Ye've lived with the woman for a year. Surely ye've noticed there are times she doesnae—"

"Och, of course I ken that time." Rocque shifted, uncomfortable with the topic. "She suffers fiercely with back pain then." He often pulled her against him in bed, able to easily rub her lower back with his large hands. "I just never bothered counting to tell it happens every month."

He shuddered.

Malcolm's grin grew as he shifted his weight to one side, the stick dangling forgotten. "Well, why did ye *think* she was bleeding?"

"I *assumed* I'd been too vigorous."

"What? Each time?"

Mal's voice had turned sympathetic, likely imagining Rocque blaming himself, so he scowled in response.

"Nay, eventually I realized 'twas no' my fault. Then I wondered if she'd eaten something spoiled."

"Which caused her to bleed."

His twin's voice had turned carefully bland, a sure sign he was holding back laughter.

With a muttered curse, Rocque heaved himself to his feet, making sure to stomp atop Malcolm's sketch as he limped away, his knee almost buckling at the sudden movement.

"When I asked, she told me 'tis a woman's business, and left it at that! I had nae *need* to ken she bleeds each month because she's no' carrying my bairn!" He shuddered again. " 'Tis a disgusting system."

" 'Tis a wonderful and miraculous system," Malcolm corrected. "But aye, disgusting as hell."

"Full of liquids and *feelings* and shite."

Malcolm nodded. "Likely worth it for the continuation of the human race, but I'm glad 'tis no' *us* going through it each month."

"If one of my men bled for four days straight..."

His brother heard his mutter, because Mal smiled. "Ye'd think him dying."

"Nay, I'd think him *dead*. Women are weird."

With a chuckle, the smaller man pushed himself to his feet. "Truer words were never spoken, brother."

Across the clearing, Rocque dragged his hands through his hair. Malcolm's lesson left him feeling... Well, a warrior would never admit to feeling nauseated because of a little grossness, so he wouldn't.

But slowly, a realization began to steal over him, and he dropped his hands. Merewyn wasn't barren. If she *were*, she wouldn't be worried about *counting*. And from Mal's explanation, it seemed that Merewyn *was* counting to prevent pregnancy.

Which means there was no reason to think she *couldn't* get pregnant, and he still had a chance at becoming—*oh, shite*.

He groaned against and dropped his head back, planting his hands on his hips and squeezing his eyes shut.

"She still willnae marry me."

As if Malcolm understood the unspoken explanation—and hellfire, maybe he did, the man *did* get all the intellect Rocque lacked—he called, "Why no'?"

"Because she says she'll no' marry a man who doesnae love her."

Rocque's brother was quiet for a long moment. Long enough for Rocque to open his eyes and glare at that damned squirrel, still skittering back and forth above them and likely laughing in his little squirrel language at the follies of man.

"Does that matter to ye?" Malcolm finally asked. "Would ye still want to marry her if *she* didnae love *ye*?"

"Nay!" Rocque spun around. "Aye! *Bah!*" He scrubbed his hands over his face once more, then crossed his arms to glare at his brother. " 'Tisnae important."

His twin mirrored his stance across the clearing, but when he shrugged, there was a bit of humor in his eyes.

" 'Tis important to *her*, brother. Do ye love her?"

Rocque glared.

Malcolm raised a brow in challenge.

Rocque glared harder.

Malcolm's second brow joined the first.

Damnation, if he glared any harder, Rocque worried his skull might pop out of his skin. Did his brother not understand he had no answer?

"Do ye love her?" Malcolm repeated quietly.

"How in the *fook* am I supposed to know that?" he burst out.

His brother began to chuckle.

Then the chuckles turned to laughter.

"Malcolm," Rocque growled in warning.

Shaking his head, Malcolm held up his palm while he managed to control his humor. "Peace, brother, peace." He was still smiling when he straightened and met Rocque's glare. "I apologize. This is one area I know naught about, but ye looked so—so *desperate* I couldnae contain—"

"Contain it," Rocque snapped.

Smiling, Malcolm took a deep breath. "Certainly. So." He lifted one finger and ticked another against it. "Ye dinnae ken if ye love her." Second finger. "She willnae marry her if ye dinnae." Third finger. "Ye want to marry her, aye?"

Another growl. "Aye." He couldn't imagine *not* spending the rest of his days with Merewyn.

Malcolm held up four fingers and tapped the smallest with a finger from his opposite hand. "And does she want to marry ye otherwise?"

There was naught in their shared past to indicate Merewyn *didn't* want to marry him...except for what she said last night.

Rocque blew out a frustrated breath. "No' if I dinnae love her."

Malcolm curled his fingers into a fist. "Then 'tis simple."

"*Naught* is simple," Rocque growled. "Ye've just run out of fingers."

"I have plenty more." His brother wiggled his fingers, then hooked his thumbs in his belt and cocked his head as he studied Rocque. "I can tell ye if ye love her."

Was Malcolm able to read minds? "How?"

"By asking ye the question you wouldnae answer earlier. If ye had to choose between marrying Merewyn and becoming laird, which would ye sacrifice?"

This time, Rocque didn't hesitate. "Becoming laird would mean naught without Merewyn at my side."

"So ye'd choose her even if it meant doing so would remove the chance of lairdship from yer future?"

Rocque nodded, his heart *finally* certain of one thing. "I would choose her even if it doomed me to an eternity of damnation. She is mine and I am hers. Becoming laird is nothing in comparison."

Malcolm's smile slowly bloomed. "Ye love her, brother."

Ye dinnae love me.

Rocque blinked slowly.

I love her?

His brother—the most brilliant man he knew—had deduced it, so it *must* be true.

"I love her?"

Malcolm chuckled as he crossed the clearing and laid one hand companionably on his brother's shoulder. "Ye do, Rocque. I suspect ye have for some time. Now, 'tis up to *ye* to decide what to do with that knowledge."

"What do ye mean?" Rocque shook his head, still stunned from the realization. "I love her."

Malcolm's grip tightened. "So go *tell* her, ye great clot-heid!" Then he released his brother and stepped away, still grinning. "Bathe first, because ye smell like an ox fooked a sheep, and ye look worse. And yer knee needs to soak in cold water. But then *tell her*."

Tell her tell her tell her.

Go tell her I love her.

Slowly, Rocque smiled, having forgotten all about the pain in his knee. "Tell her I love her."

With another shout of laughter, Malcolm strolled for the path back toward the keep. "Bathe first!" he called over his shoulder.

Rocque's gaze darted to the punching bag, all urge to pound something forgotten. Well he was already thinking about what it would feel like to take Merewyn in his arms after he told her he loved her. Would she cry? How long would it take her to agree to marry him?

Whirling, Rocque hobbled toward the loch, still grinning.

Tell her I love her.

Aye. He would. And she'd agree to marry him.

And everything would be well.

CHAPTER 7

HE DIDN'T COME HOME last night.

Sighing, Merewyn looked around her small cottage. Funny, it had never seemed too small when Rocque was here, although it should have. Now, she supposed she should start collecting his things to send back to the barracks.

Because he'd made it clear there was no future between them.

Last night she'd lain awake in bed, praying she'd hear him outside, or see him come through the door. Eventually she cried herself to sleep, and woke this morning to a cold bed.

Best get used to it.

He'd made his choice. All he'd had to do last night was say, "I love ye." But he couldn't, and that answered her question easily enough.

Before the tears began to fall again, Merewyn snatched her basket up from its hook by the door—Rocque had installed that hook, now that she thought of it—and stepped out into her garden. 'Twas a lovely summer afternoon, and she'd be damned if she was going to spend the rest of the day moping.

The sun was already creeping lower in the west, and with a start, she realized she'd missed both meals of the day. She still wasn't hungry, but knew she must eat dinner, for the sake of the bairn if naught else.

The bairn, who *would* know his father, even if his parents weren't married.

Even if his mother is too bloody stubborn to marry a man who doesnae love her.

Scowling at her own subconscious, she settled on her knees in front of her rosemary plant.

'Twas a sprawling monster of a plant, one which had spawned many clippings and offshoots. Half the village now had rosemary in the gardens, thanks to this plant.

As she always did, whenever she passed, Merewyn pinched a few leaves from the end of a stem, rubbing them between her fingers. Then, absentmindedly, she lifted the crushed leaves to rub behind her ear and at the hollow of her neck.

Rosemary was Rocque's favorite scent, and she always made certain he'd be able to smell it on her.

Not that it mattered anymore.

Sighing, she flicked away the leaves, reached for her shears, and began to prune. The longer stems, she'd hang to dry in her rafters. Some she'd send up to the keep for Cook to use. Some she'd bundle for burning—the smoke masked fouler scents from other herbs—or soaking in hot water. Lady Agatha used the bundles in her bath water, occasionally.

Aye, her rosemary had plenty of uses.

Plus, it was nice to be busy. Listing the uses for the bundles she was now setting aside was good for Merewyn's peace of mind.

She knelt in her garden, surrounded by green life, nurturing her *own* new life inside of her, and tried to breathe deeply and think of the future.

"Merewyn?"

The quiet call jerked her from her contemplation, and when she swung her gaze up, Jessie flinched away. The girl was standing in the shadows beside the house, her arms wrapped around her middle.

"Hello, lassie!" Merewyn straightened, brushing her palms against one another as she forced a smile for her patient. "I'm glad to see ye out of bed."

The girl didn't smile in return.

Stifling a sigh, Merewyn pushed herself to her feet, feeling guilty. She'd intended to check in on Jessie this morning, but couldn't seem to drag herself up to the keep. She'd convinced herself that since she'd just checked on the lassie yesterday, everything would be well.

Judging from the way Jessie's arms were wrapped around her middle and she hunched over as if trying to make herself look smaller, Merewyn had been wrong.

All was not well.

Her own problems pushed aside, Merewyn donned her healer's mantle as she moved toward the girl. "What's amiss, Jessie?" she called in a soothing tone, one hand reaching out to calm her. "Are ye in pain?"

"Nay," the lassie whispered.

Reaching her, Merewyn slid her hand into the girl's and slowly unfolded Jessie's arms from around her middle. Pulling her into the sunlight, Merewyn's eyes darted across the lassie's features and down her arms, looking for more signs of damage.

She saw none. Jessie's recent burns had healed well, but they had been nowhere near as terrible as the earlier burns. All that remained of the recent porridge incident was some redness across one cheek, and down one side of her throat.

Truly, she was healing wonderfully, likely not even needing the hemlock potion Merewyn had left with Moira to ease her pain. So why was she here?

"Jessie?" Merewyn asked again, gently. "Are ye well?"

"I'm aright." The girl didn't look up when she whispered, but kept her gaze locked on Merewyn's shoulder. "I just…"

When she trailed off, the healer gently tucked a finger beneath her chin and nudged it upward. "Ye can trust me," Merewyn said gently.

And that's when she saw the tears in the girl's eyes.

"Hamish came to visit me," Jessie whispered. "He said…things."

The shock of her announcement was enough that the lassie was able to pull her chin out of Merewyn's hold, and she dropped her gaze once more. But she kept explaining, thank the Saints.

"He said...he's said things to me before. About belonging to him one day, and how I'll be lucky to be his."

Merewyn wanted to hiss in disgust. Jessie was naught more than a girl! How *dare* a full-grown man—a *weasel* like Hamish—pester her like that.

"Did ye—did ye like what he said?"

Jessie's gaze flicked up quickly, then away. "Nay," she whispered, wrapping her arms around her middle again. "When he looks at me like that, he makes me feel...*dirty*."

Merewyn's palms itched; she either wanted to take Jessie into her arms in comfort, or find Hamish and slap him into next Michealmas.

She did neither, curling her hands into fists at her side. "I'm sorry, Jessie," she offered, trying to keep her tone as neutral as possible.

It must've worked, because the girl snuck another glance at her, and took a deep breath.

"Last week he found me working in the kitchens. I sleep there, near the Cook's room. He found me and told me he wanted me because I was so beautiful, and no one would treat me as well as he would." The lassie's words sped up. "I *ken* I'm no' beautiful, and I told him that. I didnae want him to touch me, then or later." She shuddered once. "I told him that too, and he said—he said..."

Big, tear-filled eyes met Merewyn's, and the healer's heart clenched.

The lassie was too young to have to learn about the ways of men. Especially snakes like Hamish Oliphant. The man was clearly manipulative and predatory. That he would approach a mere lassie, and one who had suffered so much physical trauma, made that clear.

Now that she considered things, Hamish had attempted something similar when he'd tried to court Merewyn last year. He'd told her she was the most beautiful woman he'd ever seen, and would just die if he couldn't have her.

"Have" her. He'd actually said that, as if she were some possession! Merewyn shook her head. She'd been a woman grown, confident in her own worth, and had seen Hamish's manipulations for what they were.

Jessie wouldn't.

Rocque will make him suffer.

Merewyn squeezed her eyes shut. Aye, no matter what her feelings toward Rocque at this moment, he was Hamish's commander, and could punish the man.

When she realized Jessie had trailed off, Merewyn forced her attention back to her patient. Gentling her voice, she made sure her pride for the girl came through when she praised her.

"Ye should *never* feel like ye have to allow a man to touch ye in ways ye dinnae like, Jessie. I am proud of ye for being smart enough to realize that, and to tell him so. What did he say when ye did?"

The lassie swallowed. "He said— He said I'd be sorry I turned him down. He said he'd show me how powerful he was, and how *painful* it'd be for breaking his heart like that."

Merewyn sucked in a breath. "Ye think he did what he did with the porridge—on purpose? Ye think that was—what?" Horror crept into her tone as realization dawned. "He threatened to hurt ye, and then he *did*."

Jessie's gaze dropped again, her eyes filling with tears. Merewyn wanted to comfort her, but her rage wouldn't subside long enough to gentle her tone.

"Did he touch ye?" she growled, her fingernails biting into her palms.

Jessie hesitated only a moment before jerking her chin down. "When I told him I didnae want him to touch me, he put—he put his hand on my arm, then my breast. He told me a lassie like me, with such ugly scars, would be lucky to get any kind of man, much less one as fine as him. Then he pinched me."

The bastard!

Seething, Merewyn shook her head. "He's a manipulative shite-weasel, Jessie. He calls ye beautiful, then points out yer scars. He's telling ye anything he thinks will convince ye to let him touch ye. I am *glad* ye told him no. What did ye do when he pinched ye?"

"I—Naught." The lassie tucked her chin against her chest. "I just stood there, and he told me I'd be sorry. He said he'd hurt me, and—and—" Her words caught on a sob. "He *did.*"

"Och, sweetling," Merewyn crooned, the girl's pain overcoming her own anger.

She reached out and pulled Jessie into her arms, and let the girl cry against her shoulder.

"He will pay for hurting ye, lassie," she assured Jessie. "Did he say more of the same today? Did he—" By the Virgin, 'twas hard to ask, but as the healer, she had to know. "Did he touch ye again?"

Gulping, the girl shook her head, even though her face was pressed against Merewyn's shoulder. "Today he told me he nae longer wanted me, since I was so ugly from the new burns."

Shite-weasel was too kind a term for him. There were likely some very friendly shite-weasels out there, in comparison to the scum who would manipulate a vulnerable girl for sexual favors.

But she forced a jolly tone as she rubbed Jessie's back soothingly. "Well, thank the Lord for small favors. He'll leave ye alone now."

She tried to sound surer than she felt. But when Jessie lifted her head, her eyes were wide and watery.

"He said he nae longer wanted me, because he was going to have *ye*, Healer."

Merewyn's breath caught in her throat.

"Giving away all my secrets, slut?"

The new voice startled the women, and Merewyn jerked away from Jessie only to see Hamish standing confidently in the middle of her rosemary.

Ignoring his insult, she pushed the girl behind her. "How *dare* ye think to show yer ugly face here, Hamish Oliphant. If ye ken what's good for ye, ye'll tuck yer cowardly tail between those skinny legs of yers, and hide from Rocque."

"Rocque," the man spat, hooking his thumbs in his belt and swaggering closer, "is no' here. He slept in the barracks last night, so I assume the two of ye have had a falling out." He shook his head, tsking in false sympathy. "Which means it's *my* turn."

Trying to appear braver than she felt, Merewyn lifted her chin. "Yer turn for what?"

Lightning-fast, he lashed out and wrapped around her upper arm, jerking her towards him. "My turn to use ye, whore," he hissed.

He was bigger than her, aye, but so were most men. Rocque was twice her size, but he'd never made her feel *small*, not the way Hamish was doing now. "Let go of me!"

His fingers bit into her skin as he dragged her around to face Jessie. "This is what a real woman looks like, ye little tease. I have nae need for ye, when I have the *healer*." He gave Merewyn a little shake, then jerked his chin toward the lane. "Get out of here, lass."

Jessie's gaze found Merewyn's. "But—"

"Dinnae make me hurt ye again," he snapped. " 'Twas yer doing afore, and ye'll only bring yerself more pain if ye defy me."

What a manipulative, disgusting, abusive donkey arse! Nay, "donkey arse" was too kind as well. *Diseased* donkey arse? Rotten, diseased, pus-filled, oozing?

Aye, *oozing donkey arse* suited him.

Rolling her eyes at her own distraction, Merewyn met the girl's gaze. "Go on, Jessie. I'll be aright."

"But—"

She nodded assuringly. "Go."

Hesitating only a moment more, the girl suddenly turned and darted around the corner of Merewyn's cottage.

The healer took a deep breath, then wrenched her arm from Hamish's grip.

"You complete bastard! How could you *possibly* think 'twas acceptable to say and do those things to *any* female, much less a girl Jessie's age?" She whirled, her anger giving her courage as she jabbed a finger at Hamish's nose. "Do ye think all women have been placed on earth for *yer* enjoyment? Think ye so high and mighty? That all women would want to satisfy ye?"

He caught her finger in his grip and *squeezed* until she sucked in a breath.

"How dare ye," he hissed. "The worst of them all, and ye think to say such a thing to *me*?"

"Excuse me?" She tried to hide the pain he was causing with indignation.

Bending her finger back, he forced her to her knees. She whimpered slightly, hating being at his mercy, as her other hand clawed at his, to no avail.

"Ye think ye have any right to chastise me? *Ye*? The village *whore*?" he spat. "Spreading yer legs for that idiot? I saw what ye did for him, on yer knees in the wood. But ye have to be *forced* to yer knees for a far superior man like me?"

Blessed Virgin, Hamish had followed them last night? He'd seen her touching herself as Rocque spilled his seed across her face and chest? But...being on her knees in front of Rocque was about power and control and—and—and *love,* damnation and hellfire! Rocque would *never* make her feel weak or unworthy, never force her or manipulate her into doing something she didn't want to do.

Because Rocque was a good man.

And because he cared for her.

In that moment, on her knees in her garden, at the mercy of an evil man, she realized that truth. Rocque *did* care for her.

He showed it in the way he treated her, in the way he held her and touched her. He showed it in the way he asked her opinion and listened, and the way he fixed little things around the cottage, and the way he smiled at her as if she were the most important thing in his world.

He cared for her.

And last night, she'd pushed him away.

Tears sprang to her eyes—tears of pain, aye, but frustration and sorrow. She'd pushed him away, and that's why she was at Hamish's mercy now.

Above her, he grinned evilly. "Ye understand now, whore! Ye understand *I* am yer master now, eh?" He bent her finger further, and pain shot up her arm as she scrambled fruitlessly to free herself. "Ye think I would just *forget* the way ye humiliated me?"

"How—How did I humiliate ye?" she gasped.

"Ye had the gall to turn me away, to pretend to be so high and mighty, only to turn around and fook *him*. That idiot with more muscle than brains!"

She'd turned down plenty of men over the years. Some she hadn't, true, which gave others the impression she was available for their pleasure. But she'd never considered that one might hold a grudge this long.

"Rocque is a good man," she managed, blinking away her tears. "He willnae let ye get away with hurting Jessie."

Or me, she added silently. Because even if she'd completely ruined her chances with Rocque, she knew he was a good enough man to punish evil-doers—

With his free hand, Hamish slapped her—hard—across her mouth, releasing his hold on her finger long enough for her to fall to the ground.

She lifted her hand to her cheek and saw him raise his fist.

Dear God above, the bairn!

She gasped as a new worry coursed through her. If Hamish hurt her here, the way he'd hurt Jessie, would he harm the babe she protected in her womb? Would she lose Rocque's bairn?

"What do ye want?" she blurted, hoping to forestall his violence.

It worked. He paused, his fist raised, and his lips pulled into a smirk. "Willing to bargain now, eh?" His chuckle was pure evil. "I should've kenned a whore like ye would rather give me what I want than be hurt." He spat at her feet. "Ye're all alike."

Terror iced her limbs as she realized he meant there were other women in his past, women he'd done this same thing to.

"What—what are ye going to do?" she whispered.

In a flash, he had grabbed a fistful of curls and dragged her to her knees. She couldn't stop the whimper from escaping her lips, but steeled herself for whatever was to come.

But instead of lifting his kilt, Hamish thrust his face toward hers, his leer as disgusting as his breath.

"He thinks he's so important, because his Da's the laird," he sneered. "He thinks that gives him the right to hit me—*me*! But he's naught but a bastard, the son of a whore like ye."

When he gave his fist a little shake, Merewyn winced, feeling her hair ripping from her scalp.

"I'm going to have ye, slut. Ye spread yer legs for him, and ye'll do the same for me. And he'll *ken* it. Will he want ye back?" His bark of laughter was harsh, and he didn't wait for a response. "But no' here. I dinnae want ye *here*, where anyone can hear ye cries of pain."

Pain?

Blessed Virgin, protect me! Protect my bairn!

"Come along, whore," he growled, tugging her toward the garden gate.

She shuffled forward on her knees, but when he yanked upward, she rose to her feet, still bent awkwardly, terror beating in her veins.

That's when he pulled a long, wicked-looking dagger from his belt and pressed it into her side as he released her hair.

"We're going for a walk, just ye and me." His tone turned conversational as he pressed against her, his body hiding the dagger at her side, and urged her out into the lane.

She looked about frantically, but saw none of the villagers out and about this late in the afternoon. Even if they saw her, they'd likely think naught of the healer walking with an Oliphant, even if Hamish *was* standing too close to be proper.

His grating chuckle told her he was counting on it. "I've wanted to fook ye for years. But if ye think to cry out, whore, I'll pierce ye with a different kind of blade, eh?"

He laughed at his own joke, and she pressed her lips together in a thin line.

When he turned his gaze back to her, she saw him licking his lip, as if she were a—a sweetmeat or some such.

"We're going into the wood, aye?" he rasped. "And when we get there, ye're going to lie down on yer back and do all those things ye've done for that idiot over the last year. He's half the man I am, so I want to hear *twice* the pleased sounds come from yer lips."

His gaze dropped to her lips. "And if I dinnae like what I hear, I'll hurt ye in ways ye cannae imagine."

And even though Merewyn *knew* there was no way for Rocque to know she was in trouble, no way to know how desperate she was, she found herself praying for him.

I am sorry I dinnae believe ye! I am sorry I dinnae tell ye about the bairn! Please, please find us!

But as Hamish jerked her into motion once more, she bit her lower lip to contain her sobs.

Rocque couldn't hear her plea.

He wasn't coming for her.

CHAPTER 8

HIS HAIR WAS STILL DRIPPING from his soak in the loch as he strode through the village. Well, mayhap not *strode*; his knee still twinged every time he put weight on that leg.

But he was off to declare his love for Merewyn, and he damn well wasn't going to *limp* up to her!

So, not-quite-hobbling, he hurried toward her cottage.

Their cottage.

In the garden, he stopped and took a deep breath. *Rosemary.* Quite a lot of it, as if someone had trampled the plant. But he didn't know enough about herbs—or gardens—to know what it was supposed to look like. 'Twas likely just that she'd been out here cutting some—

Ah! There were some clippings she'd left on the ground beside her valuable shears.

Scooping them up, he headed for the front door, and only hesitated a moment before sticking his head inside.

"Mere?" Should he have knocked? "Merewyn, love?"

She wasn't there.

Frowning now, he stepped into the house and laid her shears on the table, looking around. Everything looked in order. Mayhap she'd been in the garden and been called away by an urgent need?

If she were tending one of the villagers, he shouldn't bother her, but he couldn't ignore the nagging feeling that he needed to find her.

And not just because he wanted to confess his love, Nay.

His frown still in place, he stepped out into the garden and looked up and down the lane. This late in the day there were few people about to ask.

Mayhap she's gone to check on Jessie or Agatha!

Aye, that would be likely, and 'twould be convenient if she were up at the keep. He wouldn't feel as if he were interrupting her work, if she was checking on one of his family members.

He headed for the keep, but that nagging feeling wouldn't go away, and he was surprised to find himself jogging in his hurry to find her.

A few of his men stopped when they saw him running—hiding the wince of pain each step caused—but he waved away their concern. 'Twas a lover's quarrel, nothing more.

Right?

He didn't bother going up the main stairs to the great hall, but instead jogged around to the kitchen entrance and pushed his way through the narrow opening. "Jessie?"

Moira was speaking with Cook, and she whirled, her hand going to her chest. "Rocque, ye startled us!"

"Apologies," he murmured, already poking his head into the little room behind the hearth. "Is Merewyn here with Jessie?"

Moira shook her head. "I haven't seen either. Merewyn gave Jessie the approval to go back to work yesterday, and she was a big help this morning. Mayhap she went on a walk before the evening meal?"

The news gave Rocque pause. If Jessie was back to work, then Merewyn likely hadn't been here today. His lips tugged down thoughtfully, and he glanced around at the rest of the servants in the kitchens.

"Have any of ye seen Merewyn?"

His question was met with shakes of heads and murmured denials.

Nodding his appreciation, he headed for the stairs up to the main hall. That nagging feeling wouldn't go away.

He needed to find Merewyn and tell her he loved her!

He needed to find her and make sure she was safe.

Where had that thought come from?

He wasn't quite jogging, but by the time he crossed the main hall and headed for the bedchamber level—going to check with Aunt Agatha—no one could doubt he was in a hurry.

"Rocque!"

At his sister's call, he halted so suddenly she took a step back. They were in the upper hall, and she was grinning too broadly to have information he needed.

"Hello, Nessa," he muttered, trying to step around her.

But she stopped him again with a hand resting on his arm. "Rocque, I've been meaning to speak with ye. Aunt Agatha is helping me with my latest piece, and now I need yer help as well."

Stifling a sigh, he took a deep breath and nodded down at her. Nessa was always asking him about one thing or another, when it came to historical weaponry. Which was silly, because Malcolm was clearly the scholar in the family.

"Aye, what is it?" he asked through gritted teeth.

With a happy smile, she stepped back again and bent her knees, raising her arms to shoulder height. "I'm portraying the siege at Berwick, ye ken, and I have a pikeman. Would he stand like this?" She thrust her arms out, as if holding an imaginary stick. "Or like this?" Twisting her upper body, she jabbed to the side.

He winced. *Both* stances were laughably wrong, but how hard would it be to portray them in embroidery?

"Try this." He lifted one of her elbows and nudged her hips into a different position, then stepped back for a hurried examination.

She still looks like a bugler mid-way through a whiskey tasting, no' a pikeman. Pikewoman? Bah.

Giving up, he shook his head. "Ye have nae idea how to hold a weapon, do ye?"

"'Tis what she said!"

He rolled his eyes and stepped back. "I see ye've been speaking with Kiergan."

"Aye, 'tis a delightful addition to my humorous repertoire. I cannae wait to use it on whichever Henry Da betroths me to next."

St. John's elbows! He didn't have *time* for this!

Craning his head around his sister, he glanced up and down the hall, hoping Merewyn would step out of Agatha's room. "I'm sure yer future husband will appreciate ye're understanding of crude jokes."

"He'll appreciate my understanding of crude *acts* even more!" she giggled.

Frowning, Rocque pinned her with a glare. "*What* did ye just say?"

"Och, dinnae be a hypocrite. Ye and Merewyn have been carrying on for months, and ye're no' married."

No' for lack of trying. " 'Tis different," he growled. "Merewyn is no' my little sister."

Nessa wrinkled her nose. "I should hope not. That is disgusting."

Rocque *wanted* to ask what kind of *crude acts* his little sister had knowledge of, and who taught her, but right now, he had other things on his mind. With another sigh, he scrubbed his hand over his face.

"Can we continue this conversation some other time?"

Grinning, she dropped down into the position he'd tried to show her with the imaginary pike. "It'll only take a moment. Ye think this looks better than—"

He interrupted her as he shook his head. "Remind me tomorrow, and I'll show ye with an actual pike, aye?"

"But—"

He tried to step around her again. Down the hall, Aunt Agatha's door was open. "Tomorrow, Nessa."

As he headed for the door, his sister lifted her skirts and hurried after him.

"But Rocque, I have another question!"

"Aye?" he grunted.

"Do ye think the defenders were more likely to have boiling oil or boiling pitch? I was going with oil, but it matters for my latest dye lot and—"

Stopping suddenly, he whirled around and reached for her cheeks. She was startled into silence, and he pulled her head forward to plant a kiss on her head.

"Nessa, sister, I love ye dearly. And I will answer all yer blood-thirsty, inappropriate questions, I swear. But for now, I have to find Merewyn."

She gasped and pulled out of his hold. "Are ye sick?"

"Nay." Then he chuckled. "Aye!" Lovesick, mayhap. "Is she with Aunt Agatha?"

"Rocque, I—"

But he wasn't sure what she was planning on saying, because he'd stepped through the open door to his aunt's chambers. "Aunt Agatha?"

The old woman was bent over in front of her chair, struggling with something. But when she heard him, she whirled about with a gasp.

"Rocque! Thank God ye're here!"

That nagging worry—worry for Merewyn—slammed back into him, and his eyes darted around the chamber even as his aunt hobbled toward him. Merewyn wasn't here, but Agatha's foot was bandaged. Had she seen his love recently?

"What is it?" he asked hoarsely.

Agatha's eyes were bright as she juggled her bundle. "I need ye, Rocque! Desperately. Ye are the only one who can do this for me!"

His heart down somewhere near his stomach, Rocque swallowed and stepped for his aunt, reaching to help her. "What do ye need? What is it?"

"Here, lad, hold yer hands like this."

The old woman took his hands, already outstretched, and moved them shoulder-width apart, with his palms facing one another. While he was frowning in confusion, she nodded smartly and dropped most of the bundle in her arms.

As Rocque watched the threads—skeins?—hit the ground, she tucked one end of a wool thread between two of his fingers as an anchor and began to twist them, first across the back of one hand, then the other, in a circle.

He blinked. "Aunt Agatha?"

Humming, she concentrated on her task, her gnarled hands flying as she wrapped the blue thread around his hands.

"What do ye need me to do?"

"Ye're doing it, lad!"

Rocque squinted down at his hands, watching her loop the thread. "Ye needed me to...what?"

"To stand there, verra still, and let me wind my threads in place!" She snapped. "Of course, they're really *Nessa's* threads, I suppose. Still, I cannae wind them around my *own* hands, can I? Dinnae be silly."

Agatha didn't need *him*. She just needed a pair of hands. Irritated now, he started to step back, but she slapped him on the arm.

"Stand still! I swear, lad, ye're green as a turnip top, and about as popular."

He opened his mouth, but no sound came out.

What in damnation is that supposed to mean?

"Aunt Agatha," he began, his tone pitched in warning, "I am needed elsewhere."

She didn't need him, but Merewyn might.

But she just scoffed. "I need ye here, lad."

"Ye have a perfectly good set of hands."

She made a little snorting sound. " *'Tis what she said."*

And Rocque, having learned his lesson out in the corridor, pressed his lips together and rolled his eyes up toward the ceiling, refusing to be sucked into a *'Tis what she said* conversation with another female relative.

Agatha, clearly thinking she'd won, continued happily. "Yer hands are the perfect space apart, and ye're the only one I can talk into standing still long enough to help me." She shook her head. "Pretty as a turnip green, dumb as the root."

Aright, *that* one he understood.

He frowned, used to being called dumb, but not needing this right now. He turned, and quick as a flash, she'd grabbed a pinch of skin on his forearm between two fingers and *squeezed*.

"Ow!" he jerked away. "What in hellfire was that for?"

"To make ye stay *still*, lad! We're almost done," she scolded as she slid the thread through her fingers. "Remember, turnips don't mind bein' rooted up, they're just glad to be useful!"

"Agatha," he growled, "just what is going on with ye and turnips?"

The old woman flashed blue eyes up at him and scowled. "I'm hungry, aright?"

He watched her deftly wind the blue thread around his hands, and came to two important realizations. One: she wasn't going to let him go until the bloody thread was bloody well done. And two: He respected her too much to yank the thread from his hands, drop it to the floor, and stomp—limp?—out of here.

No matter how much he wanted to.

Stifling another sigh, he realized he was stuck here for the duration.

"Och, well," he muttered, "ye could talk the ears off a turnip."

She stopped what she was doing—damnation!—to blink up at him. "Turnips dinnae have ears, lad."

"So?"

"So, it doesnae make any sense!"

He snorted softly, but managed not to snap, *And the shite ye say does make sense?*

Instead, he jerked his chin toward the pile of blue still tangled on the floor. "Get on with it. Please."

The old woman clicked her tongue softly, but focused on her task once more. "Ye're certainly in a hurry to get out of here, lad."

"I have to find Merewyn."

She was likely fine—safe—at some villagers' home. So why this nagging feeling of worry?

"Merewyn, eh?" His great-aunt hummed thoughtfully. "Are ye ill?"

He watched the pile of thread dwindling as it wrapped around his hands, trying to calculate how much longer he'd have to stand here. "I just need to see her. Are ye almost done?"

"Laddie, a flood can uncover turnips, but that doesnae make them ripe."

Rocque frowned down at the top of her head. Had she called him a turnip again? Or was she just hungry?

Nay, 'twas something about not rushing things, he was certain...

"Are ye insulting me again, Aunt?"

She tsked, her eyes still on her job. "I've never insulted ye. If ye grown down a turnip, ye'll grow up a flower."

His breath burst out of him in exasperation and he yanked his hands away. "What in *damnation* is that supposed to mean?"

Scowling, she brandished two fingers. "Dinnae make me pinch ye again, laddie!" she snapped. Then her expression softened slightly, and she tugged his hands back into position. "I'm almost done."

He glanced at the door—freedom was so close!—but she was right. The end of the blue thread *was* approaching, judging from the dwindling pile on the floor.

She worked in silence for a moment, then hummed again.

"Looking for Merewyn, eh, laddie? Have ye heard the drummer lately?"

What did that have to do with anything? "Aye," he admitted cautiously. "I heard him last night, since I slept in the barracks."

His great aunt cackled gleefully. "Slept in the barracks, did ye? Trouble with yer love, is there?"

He pressed his lips closed, unwilling to admit to anything.

She was still chuckling when she glanced up at him and shook her head. "Rocque, my lad, ye're a good man. Dense as a turnip sometimes, but a good man. Hearing the drummer means ye're already *doooomed*."

"Doomed to fall in love, aye." Rocque shook his head. "We've all heard yer theory, Aunt."

" 'Tis nae theory, laddie!"

"Then why have *ye* no' fallen in love?" he snapped in return; his brow raised.

For the first time ever, he saw his great-aunt flustered. "Och, well... We're no' speaking of *me*!"

The end of the thread was in her grasp, but she held on to it. Purposefully, if he didn't miss his guess.

She brandished the end at him like a weapon. "We're speaking of *ye*, Rocque. Ye've heard the drummer. Yer healer has heard the drummer."

Merewyn heard the Ghostly Drummer of Oliphant Castle? His other brow joined the first.

And his aunt nodded proudly. "Ye love her, do ye no'?"

Slowly, his expression eased into a smile. "I do." He might not have realized it until this afternoon—thanks to Malcolm—but now he'd yell it from the rooftops. Or take up drumming along with the ghost. "I love her."

Deftly, she wound the end of the thread around the skein he'd made with his hands. "Then why have ye no' told her, ye turnip head?"

As he finally—*finally!*—pulled his hands from the thread, he couldn't contain the chuckle which burst forth. "Why do ye think I'm *looking for her*, Aunt?"

His great aunt blinked, and he liked knowing *he'd* surprised her for a change.

"Och, well…" She waved her hand grandly toward the hall. "What are ye waiting on? Go on!"

Thankfully, he offered he a little bow and darted for the door. But he stuck his head back in. "Oh, Aunt Agatha?"

She startled, looking up from her skein. "What?" she snapped.

He grinned. "I hope ye find something to eat soon. Some turnips, mayhap?"

"Turnips?" She scowled and made a rude gesture. "Get out of here!"

Gladly.

Chuckling, he ducked back into the hall.

But his humor had fled by the time he reached the main hall. Moira already had the servants bustling about, preparing for dinner, and no one he'd asked had seen Merewyn.

He wasn't sure why his heart was pounding so hard, worrying him about her. 'Twas as if, now that he was determined to declare his love for her, he had to do it *now*. Or risk what? She'd be home soon enough, likely, and he could tell her then.

That logic didn't seem to help his heart, though.

If naught else, he could wait for her at her—*their* cottage.

"Rocque, are things well?" Brohn called, concern in his voice as he jogged to catch up with Rocque.

Without stopping, Rocque jerked his head to indicate the other man should walk with him. "Merewyn is—well, she's no' exactly missing, but I cannae find her, and I have a bad feeling..."

His soon-to-be second slapped him on the shoulder with a nod. "Trust yer instincts, Commander. I'll start some men asking around."

Distractedly, Rocque nodded in appreciation. "Report yer findings. I'm heading back to her cottage."

As Brohn jogged toward the barracks, Rocque trotted down the keep's front steps and into the bailey, wondering if he should ask Merewyn to tend to his bruised knee. *After* he told her he loved her.

And asked her to marry him again.

"Milord?"

He almost didn't hear the quiet call, and even then, considered ignoring it in his haste to reach the cottage.

When he whirled about, he forced his scowl to soften as he recognized the speaker. Wee Jessie huddled in the shadows.

"Aye, lassie?" He tried to keep his voice soft, and his impatience out of his tone.

From the way she twitched, he might not have accomplished that.

"Milord, I've been looking... I didnae ken who else to find..."

What was she doing out of bed? Were those—were those *tear tracks* on her cheeks?

"What is it?" He knew his tone was harsh, but now he had another female to worry about. "Are ye hurt? Did—Damn and blast, did Hamish hurt ye again?"

"Nay, but..." When she stepped out of the shadows, he saw the tears in her eyes, saw the way she held herself. "He's hurting her, milord. Merewyn."

Rocque lunged for the girl, but even as he grabbed her shoulders, he realized he was frightening her. He couldn't seem to make himself let her go, but at least he didn't shake her, as he wanted. Instead, he bent over, meeting her eyes.

"Hamish is hurting Merewyn?" he clarified, his voice dangerous.

She winced, but nodded. "Aye, milord. He found me today, and he told me—he told me he was going to make her pay. I found her, and told her." Jessie swallowed, and met his eyes. "Then he arrived and made me leave."

St. John's sacred forelock! "Hamish is alone with her? Are they at the cottage? And what did he mean—make her pay?"

There were tears spilling down Jessie's cheeks now, and he tried to loosen his hold, afraid he was hurting her. But by all the saints in Heaven, he needed the answers!

His heart pounded frantically, torn between ripping his sword free and chasing after Hamish, and getting all the information he could ahead of time.

"I—I—" She took in great, heaving breaths of air. "I didnae go, milord! I hid around the corner and I listened!"

Oh, thank fook.

"What did he said, Jessie?" he whispered.

"Hamish said he wanted her, and never forgave her for rejecting him, then going with *ye*. He said he was angry at ye for hitting him—he said terrible things, about ye, milord, but I didnae believe him, and neither did Merewyn. We ken ye're a fine man, and—"

This time, he did shake her, just a bit. He needed to know what to expect. "Are they at the cottage, Jessie?"

She shook her head, eyes wide among her scars, and his heart fell.

"Where are they?" he whispered.

"I dinnae ken, milord. But he put a dagger in her side and walked down the lane toward the wood. He was speaking about what he saw the two of ye doing last night, among the trees? Is that where he's going?"

Hellfire and damnation!

Hamish had spied upon them last night?

If so, and if he was so disgusting as to take Merewyn—to hurt her —just because she refused him...then Rocque knew where they were going.

With a whispered curse, he straightened.

It would take time to rouse his men, time he didn't have.

And he didn't need them, not truly.

Hamish was just one man. A weasel of a man, true, but he had no friends. No men who would follow him.

He had dared to touch—to threaten—the woman Rocque loved, and he would not live through the night.

And if he'd *hurt* Merewyn, then God help him, because Hamish wouldn't even have time to make peace with his Creator before Rocque killed him with his bare hands.

CHAPTER 9

'Twas almost full dark by the time they reached the little clearing in the wood, where Merewyn had lain with Rocque. Had it only been last night? So much had changed in such a short amount of time.

And now, Hamish yanked her hard enough to cause her to stumble as they stepped into the clearing. His hand closed tightly around her upper arm, and she knew she'd have bruises there.

"Ah, here we are," he crowed, shoving her forward.

She stumbled and hit the ground on her hands and knees, but truthfully, was just pleased to no longer have that blade in her side. She'd spent the last mile waffling between deliberately dragging her feet and hoping someone would notice them, and fearing for her life if he grew irritated.

Hamish, on the other hand, seemed to grow bolder the farther they got from the village. Or mayhap 'twas the closer they got to this clearing. Even now, he strutted toward the small brook, his shoulders back as he gestured with his blade.

"I like the way ye look on yer hands and knees, whore. I liked it last night, too. Shall I tell ye how I fooked my own fist, standing there in the shadows, and pretended 'twas yer face I spilled over? Ye looked up at that bastard lover of yers and took all of *his* seed, so I kenned ye'd take mine!"

Shuddering, Merewyn rolled to sit, pulling her knees to her chest and wrapping her arms around them. The idea of Hamish *watching* her and Rocque doing something so intimate…'twas disgusting. And disturbing.

And scary.

She shivered again, and realized how cold she really was. 'Twas summer, aye, but the nights were still chilled, and she didnae have her shawl.

" 'Tis good ye're scared, whore. Ye *should* be scared. 'Tis only because I havenae tired of ye that ye still live."

Merewyn's eyes rounded. Blessed Virgin, he intended to…to what? To use her, then kill her?

She swallowed. If he killed her, her babe died as well.

If she and the bairn died, Rocque would never know she loved him. Never know she was carrying his babe. Never know how much she wanted to be his, and only his.

Too bad ye were too stubborn to admit it last night.

Tightening her hold on her knees, she did her best to suppress her shivers. If she wanted to stay alive, she needed to *not* irritate Hamish. She needed him to want to keep her alive.

And while she wasn't planning on willingly submitting to him, she could at least stop goading him.

"I'm—I'm just a little cold," she admitted through chattering teeth.

Cold, aye, but fear made her shiver as well.

But the way he clucked his tongue dismissively told her she'd guessed correctly.

"I should've kenned a wee whore like ye wouldnae be able to handle a night like this without a *man* to keep ye warm. 'Tis why ye needed that bastard last night, and while ye'll welcome me soon enough."

She pressed her lips together to keep from speaking in Rocque's defense again. She didn't need another bruise to match the one on her cheek and arm.

He sighed and waved his blade toward the deadfall along the

banks of the stream. "But first, aye, ye can make a fire if ye're so chilled. I'll no' have ye touching me with cold hands."

Slowly, she unfolded herself. "Truly?"

If she could make a fire, mayhap 'twould signal other Oliphants. Or mayhap she'd be able to use a burning log as a weapon or something!

When he merely grunted and waved her toward the sticks, she scrambled to her feet.

"But dinnae think to escape me, whore. I am twice yer size, and a faster runner. If I have to chase ye down, I *will* hurt ye." He nodded solemnly; a glint of madness visible in his eyes even in the dimming light.

Dear God in Heaven, she would have to take him down hard if she had the chance. She couldn't just hit him and run; she'd have to hit him and hurt him.

She was a healer. Could she do that? Could she purposefully hurt another human?

To save my bairn, aye.

So she lifted her chin and met his eyes, hiding her shudder. "A fire will warm us both," was all she said.

Feeling his eyes on her the whole time, she went to gather firewood. As the light grew dimmer, she realized she could use the fire as an excuse to stall. Not that she was certain *what* she was stalling for, but mayhap something would come to her. All she knew was that if she was still building the fire, he couldn't rape her.

So she took her time, sorting the sticks by size, taking as much time as she dared to lay them in piles based on their thickness or length, being careful to select only the driest logs.

He might've gotten irritated with her, but to her surprise, didn't. Nay, he took the time to *talk*.

He told her everything he planned do to do her. It ranged from the grotesque—involving excrement and odd sexual fetishes—to the mundane. He described the life they'd lead, in her cozy little cottage, with him bringing home meat and her caring for his every whim.

The picture he painted made her want to weep, because it was so different from what she shared with Rocque. Rocque *respected* her, cared enough about her to consider her feelings before making requests—never demands.

He might not love her, but what he felt for her was close enough, Merewyn was certain.

As she knelt in the center of the clearing, hands shaking as she tried to stack the kindling just so, she found herself praying.

Blessed Virgin mother, please grant me the chance to tell Rocque I love him. Please let me have the chance to say aye *to him. Please let him still want me after Hamish is done with me!*

Swallowing, she opened her eyes and blew out a breath.

He was still speaking, but she had a job to do.

The spark caught easily, and soon her little blaze was merrily lighting a small area around her.

"Good," he crowed proudly, his teeth, eyes, and blade gleaming in the reflected light. "Now make it bigger. Ye're nae longer shivering—see, I notice *everything* about ye, whore—but I want to be able to *see* ye."

Without speaking, she reached for a larger piece of wood. It suited her to have a larger fire as well—more chance of being seen, if anyone was looking, and mayhap she could use the fire as a weapon of some sort?

But he must've misinterpreted the look she'd given him.

"Dinnae think to sass me!" he growled, stepping toward her and waggling the dagger in her direction. "I can hurt ye without breaking ye, remember that. Ye think I dinnae need a bigger fire to see ye, when I can see ye well enough now?"

She shook her head. "Nay, I wasnae—"

"Dinnae interrupt me! I can see ye now, aye, but I want to be able to see *all* of ye. And I want ye to be warm."

The way he was staring at her—was he drooling?—had Merewyn's pulse thumping in her temples. "W—why?" Why did he care if she was warm?

"Keep building that fire, whore! Bigger!" he chortled gleefully.

Blessed Virgin, was he mad? He must be!

As quick as possible, she began tossing logs onto the fire she'd made. They were dry and caught easily. He kept yelling "Bigger!" so she tossed on as many as she could before the heat became too intense and she had to scramble backward.

Her skirts caught under her heel and she tipped onto her arse. She laid there, arms braced, legs splayed, watching him wide-eyed through the flames. His grin was manic as he stalked toward her.

"There now, we cannae have ye catching fire," he crooned, almost gently, as he yanked her to her feet. His tone was juxtaposed with his grip, and she winced.

When he pulled her against him, and dropped his face to her neck, her stomach churned at his breath. Or maybe it was fear, making her nauseated. The fire was bright and hot at her back, so she couldn't flinch away, as much as she wanted to.

Instead she closed her eyes and sent a silent prayer for strength heavenward.

She was pressed against his body, a mockery of the embraces she'd shared with Rocque. But whereas Rocque's size had always made her feel protected, Hamish…Hamish made her feel weak.

She *hated* feeling weak.

Twisting her face away from his, she opened her eyes and unerringly found the last log she'd placed. It wasn't in the fire, but close enough that the tip was smoldering. It would catch soon, and it would be the only weapon she had.

"Take off yer dress."

She wasn't sure she'd heard his murmur correctly, but when she felt his tongue slither up the side of her neck, she shuddered.

"Never mind, I'll do it for ye."

And the blade in his hand pierced the wool of her gown, slicing it up toward her breasts.

She didn't have time to flinch away, before the dagger flashed away again, and slowly, her bodice gaped open. He'd cut through her chemise as well, and she'd barely noticed the rush of cold night air against her breast before one of his hands closed greedily over it.

"So good," he moaned, squeezing harshly.

She sucked in a gasp—both at the invasion of his touch and at the suddenness of it all—but that only caused him to chuckle and move his hand to the other breast.

"Does that hurt, whore?" He squeezed again, and she managed not to whimper. "I *want* it to hurt. But no' yet, no' yet." He shook his head, squeezing again. "Ye'll hurt later. And now. And later."

As he cackled, she felt a part of her, deep inside, shrivel. He *was* mad.

And she was alone with him.

With a sudden yank, he ripped her gown from her shoulder, and she stumbled forward as the thing tore down the middle and down over her arms.

"Take it off!" he commanded, stepping away from her. He gestured with his blade. "Strip that dress off and toss it in the fire."

Her eyes widened. "Why?"

"Ye'll be warm enough when I'm done with ye!" he laughed again. "Take it off and burn it, and then ye'll get on yer knees. I'll start by using yer mouth the way that bastard did! And when I spread my seed all over ye, it'll drip down yer skin and ye'll be *mine!*"

God in Heaven, help me!

But there was no alternative. And with him waving that dagger, she could only take her time and pray he wouldn't get irritated.

Slowly, she pulled her ripped gown over her other arm, then stepped out of it. She still wore her stockings, slippers and chemise, although the linen gaped in the front from his blade. Still, it hid her body from his gaze, and although she saw him greedily eyeing her form, it was a comfort.

For now.

"Into the fire with it! Do it!"

Swallowing, Merewyn sidestepped toward the blaze, eyeing him warily. As she watched, he shifted his dagger to his left hand—the one he'd pawed her with—and reached up under his kilt with the other.

His tongue flicked out over his lips as he began stroking himself, and Merewyn shuddered again.

"Hurry up, whore," he rasped. "Throw that away and get rid of

that undergown! I want ye naked and on yer knees in ten seconds."
Smiling crudely, he waved the dagger and pumped his hips at her. "Or
I'll have trouble deciding which *blade* to use on ye!"

Her time had run out.

She hurried to drop the gown in the flames, which were smoth-
ered momentarily but then caught again easily. While bent over, she
reached for the log lying alongside the flames. The end had caught,
and as she moved it, the flames extinguished into embers.

Good enough.

She turned, holding the log alongside her leg, but hidden by her
body. Her best hope was to sidle up to him and swing. He'd have
plenty of time to block her blow, but she was hoping he wouldn't be
able to, with his hands full the way they were.

"I said to take the other gown off, whore," he spat. "Ye dinnae
listen well, but at least ye dinnae talk back. I'll be able to fill that
pretty mouth of yers with something *else*. Come here."

He was pumping himself now, his breaths hitching as he stroked,
and she hoped that meant he'd be distracted.

Stepping toward him, keeping the smoldering log behind her leg,
she swallowed, knowing this was her only chance.

His gaze was on her breasts, greedily panting at the way the linen
had fallen open to reveal her skin. Her breasts *had* been heavier
recently, and still hurt from his touch.

Steady, lass. For the bairn.

Taking a deep breath, she stepped up in front of him, torqued her
torso, and launched herself into motion, swinging the burning log up
and around.

Miracle of miracles, it caught him in the side of the head, and he
stumbled back, howling.

Not good enough. She needed him *down*.

So she gripped the makeshift weapon and barreled toward
Hamish, as he flailed at his hair, yelling about being burnt.

But before she could reach him, a shape rose up from behind him.

A large, dark shape.

A shape she recognized.

"Rocque!" she blurted, skidding to a stop an arm's reach from Hamish.

He froze. "Rock? Wha—"

And then his voice—and breath—was cut off when her love snaked an arm around the villain's throat.

Over Hamish's shoulder, she saw Rocque's blue eyes skim over her, saw the anger in his gaze when he hissed in Hamish's ear, "Ye'll never again hurt the woman I love, ye shite-weasel."

Shite-weasel, heh. That had been what *she'd* called him, hadn't it?

Wait, *the woman I love?*

He...he loved her?

Her chest expanded as she sucked in a breath, opening her mouth to tell Rocque how she felt about *him*, and how incredibly grateful she was that he'd found her, when Hamish managed a choking laugh.

"Aye, I will, ye bastard!"

And with that, he leaned all his weight back into Rocque, swung his leg up, and kicked her in the chest.

Merewyn screamed as she flew backward, barely hearing the *crack* as Hamish's neck broke. Then she landed in the fire, the flames wrapping around her left calf. She screamed again, rolling away from the pain and the flames.

Her third scream was cut off abruptly when she felt herself flying through the air yet again. She was in his arms, and he was running.

When he dropped to his knees, she whimpered from the jostling. Her lower leg felt as if it was on fire.

Then he yanked her chemise out of the way and dropped her into the stream. He released her legs long enough to splash water over her left calf without releasing her shoulders.

Blessed Virgin, the relief was enough to bring tears to her eyes.

Or maybe that was gratitude.

Her hands clutched his plaid, pulling him closer. Although, given their relative sizes, she only succeeded in pulling herself against *his* chest.

"Shh, lass, I have ye," he whispered, his voice sounding strange.

When she peered up at him, she couldn't see his expression,

because the fire lit his back. He was intent on her leg, and wasn't looking at her anyhow.

Why? Was he...what did he think happened?

"He didn't hurt me," she managed to choke out. Around Rocque's arm, she could see Hamish's body, sprawled limply beside the fire. "He didnae—"

"He hurt ye," Rocque interrupted, his gentle touch as he examined her leg at odds with the hardness in his voice. "He hurt ye because I wasn't here."

"He didnae r-rape me." Now that the danger had passed, she felt herself beginning to shake. Or mayhap 'twas because of the cold water she was all-but-sitting in. "He touched me, but naught—"

With a violent curse, Rocque swept her up into his arms again, not seeming to care that the water dripped on him. He crushed her to his chest, but that didn't seem to stop her shivers.

"St. John's warts, Mere. I will never forgive myself."

Now her breaths were coming in great, heaving gasps. "For—for what?" she managed, pressed against him.

Kneeling there on the forest floor, he yanked her away from his chest to press his forehead against hers. "I should've been with you."

"My—my fault," was all she could manage.

It *had* been her fault. If she hadn't pushed Rocque away last night —in this very clearing—Hamish wouldn't have found her alone.

Thoughts of what could've happened started her shivering again. And although she knew 'twas just shock, she couldn't help wrapping her arms around her stomach and pressing against him.

The danger was over, but she didn't want him to stop protecting her. Or the bairn.

"Merewyn," he groaned, genuine sorrow in his voice as he pressed his lips to her temple. "Love, I'll never let ye come to harm, I swear it."

Love.

He'd said he loved her, didn't he?

She wanted to ask him, but as soon as she realized it, her shivers stopped. It was as if her entire body relaxed, and as her breathing slowed, her eyelids grew heavy.

Her leg was blessedly numb—although as soon as the cold wore off, she knew it would hurt fiercely. But at that moment, she was comfortable, in his arms.

So comfortable...

She tilted her head back to stare up at his profile, all she could see in the darkness.

Ye care about me.

It wasn't until she saw the flash of his teeth in his beard that she knew she'd whispered the words out loud.

He pressed a kiss to her forehead. "Forever and always, love."

Exhaling in satisfaction, she closed her eyes.

Everything will be aright, she thought to her bairn.

And then all she knew was blackness.

CHAPTER 10

ROCQUE WAS careful not to jostle her leg as he rushed back toward the village, but he couldn't help squeezing Merewyn against his chest and thanking St. John with every other breath.

I was almost too late.

As long as he lived, he didn't think he'd forget the terror which had hit him when he'd heard what Hamish had planned. The shite-weasel had threatened to kill her after raping her?

Nay, "shite-weasel" was too kind a term for Hamish, but Rocque couldn't think of anything better.

What would he have done had Jessie not stayed to overhear where Hamish was taking Merewyn? *She* was the real hero here. Rocque's heart had been in his throat as he'd all but ran to the clearing where Merewyn had left him last night, but he'd forced himself to slow, to *listen*.

And what he'd heard had been bad enough, but not as bad as seeing little Merewyn, the woman he loved, scoop up a burning log to use against Hamish.

As soon as he'd realized her intent, Rocque had wished he could roar in defiance, draw Hamish's attention to keep her out of danger.

But he'd also known he was too far away to help, and he could use Merewyn's distraction to get closer. So although it had damn well killed him to stay quiet, he'd waited until her blow had forced Hamish closer, then grabbed him.

At first, Rocque had intended to use his blade on the shite-weasel. Or whatever piece of filth Hamish was. But in his rage, he'd reached for the villain with his bare hands, and hadn't hesitated to snap Hamish's neck.

But not before he'd hurt Merewyn one last time.

" 'Twill be aright, love," he whispered hoarsely, as much to remind himself as to reassure her, who—as near as he could tell—was still unconscious in his arms.

Nay, just fainted from the excitement and pain.

She *would* be aright. He swore it.

As he reached the village, he saw people moving about with torches, and assumed they'd been organized by Brohn. "I have her!" he bellowed, relieved to hear Merewyn moan in response. "Someone fetch Brohn to the healer's cottage!"

He didn't wait to see who was following his command, but turned down the lane and stepped into her garden. Again, the scent of rosemary rose around him, and he wondered if Hamish was responsible for the destruction in the garden he'd seen earlier.

Inside their little cottage—because it *would* be theirs, he vowed it —Rocque gently placed her on the big bed and moved the screen out of the way. She moaned again, and rolled to one side.

Wincing, he tried to pull her chemise closed, hating the reminder of Hamish's invasion. But the damage to the material was too great, and her breasts still showed through the opening. He couldn't tell if her skin was bruised, and wasn't sure she'd even want him touching her.

For now, he'd focus on what he *could* do.

What had she used on Jessie when she'd been burned? He'd watched...oh, aye, goatweed. Rocque's lips twitched when he remembered the plant's other name: St. John's wort.

St. John, help me find it now to make her healthy.

Surely he could figure out which of her dozens of pouches and jars contained that salve?

He lit some candles and stood in the center of the cottage, alternately glaring at the herbs drying above his head and the shelves of jars stored across the back wall. 'Twas almost a relief when the pounding came at the door, distracting him from his impossible task.

In two long strides, he wrenched the door open. "What?"

Brohn didn't seem offended by his bark, but peered around Rocque to look at the cottage. "Ye found her? Is she safe?"

"She is now." Blowing out a breath, Rocque scrubbed a hand over his face. "Hamish had her."

"God in Heaven," Brohn whispered.

"Aye." Rocque straightened and gave a nod to the man he already thought of as his second. "His body is in the wood, and near as I can tell, he acted alone. A twisted, sick mind."

Brohn was nodding. "Revenge then?"

Not wanting to go into all the details, Rocque's answering nod was curt. "Aye. I'll see to Merewyn now, and will give ye the details in the morning."

The man—not much smaller than Rocque himself—clasped Rocque's forearm. They'd been raised together, and trusted one another to do what was right.

"Dinnae lose her," Brohn murmured, his eyes darting to the bed once more.

For the first time in what seemed like forever, Rocque grinned. "I dinnae intend to."

As he shut the door behind Brohn, he heard her whisper.

"Ye're no' going to tell him what he—what he did?"

His heart leapt, hearing her voice, but he forced himself to take a deep breath and remain at the door. He *wanted* to rush to her, to crush her against his chest, but he didn't want to frighten—or hurt—her.

So he just shook his head once, curtly. "Nae one needs to ken, if ye dinnae want them to. Tomorrow I'll tell Brohn and Da what they ask, and I willnae lie, but if ye ask me to—"

"I dinnae mind." She rolled to her back and planted her palms by her side. "They need to ken he was a complete—what an utter..."

"Shite-weasel?" he offered.

She made a little snorting sound which might've been an attempt at a laugh as she pushed herself up. " 'Tis too kind a word. He was scum, and I'm *glad* he's dead, although as a healer, I'm supposed to care for my clan."

When he realized she was struggling to rise, he hurried to her side, dropped to his knee beside the bed, and gently pushed against her shoulder.

"Be still, love. Nae one would ever begrudge ye feeling relief at Hamish's death," he muttered distractedly, reaching for her chemise's hem. "Now, I ken ye're in pain, so lie still."

When he gently pulled the linen off her leg, they both hissed. Luckily, it hadn't stuck in the wound, but the movement must have pained her as much as it pained him to make it.

"Ach, love, 'tis a nasty burn." Swallowing down nausea at the thought of her agony, he stood. "Where do ye keep the goatweed?"

She blinked up at him. "Ye remember what I use on burns?"

He was already peering at the pouches of powders she had lined up on a shelf by the door. "Aye, ye mixed it with animal fat, and spread it on Jessie's burns."

"Over there."

When he turned, he saw her nodding toward the opposite side of the cottage, so he hurried over. But he wasn't sure if she meant the jars or the bundles of herbs

Reaching up, he pulled down one and sniffed it, determined to take care of her the way she cared for so many people. The way she cared for *him.*

Hmm, that didn't smell like goatweed. How *did* goatweed smell? He reached for another, hanging the first up again. Was this what he needed? It smelled familiar…

Turning, he thrust the bundle toward her. "Is this goatweed or coriander?"

Her lips twitched upward, although she looked exhausted. "That's rosemary."

Ahh. He held out the bundle and peered at it. It didn't *look* like rosemary, but the scent... He sniffed it again. "I should've kenned. 'Tis my favorite."

"Aye," she murmured, allowing her head to fall back against the pillow. "I ken. 'Tis why I wear it."

He swung around to stare at her, and a *certainty* bloomed in his chest which had him smiling.

'Tis why I wear it.

And that's when he *knew*.

WHY WAS he looking at her that way?

Merewyn risked his irritation by pushing herself up in the bed. When he didn't say aught—just continued to stare, wide-eyed—she slid the pillows behind her so she could rest more comfortably.

God's Wounds, but her leg ached. She was hesitant to look at the burn, not wanting to see the damage, but she could sure as hellfire *feel* it. In fact, 'twas what it felt like; hellfire.

But the knowledge that he was trying to help her—he'd even remembered what herb to use!—made her feel warm inside.

He cared.

Slowly, his lips pulled upward. "Ye wear it for me?"

What had they been speaking of? Oh, aye, he'd mistaken rosemary for goatweed. Carefully, not to jar her leg, she shrugged.

"Aye, 'tis yer favorite scent. So I hang it around the cottage."

"And ye *wear* it."

Why was this so important? "I rub a bit on my skin."

His grin grew. "I love the way ye smell."

And although she expected a lascivious wink there, all he did was reach up and hang the rosemary bundle back up in the rafters, then turn toward her shelf of jars.

"Is the goatweed here?"

There was something going on in his mind, but Merewyn was too drained to figure it out. "Aye," she murmured. "Third from the left. I keep it..."

"Pre-mixed, I see," he finished, pulling the oiled skin from the lid and sniffing at it. "I just smear this on?"

"Aye, but..." She winced as she shifted her leg, turning it a bit so the burn on her calf was pointed up. "Cold water first, please."

"Och, aye!" He slapped himself on the forehead, then shook his head as he put the jar down on the table, grabbed the water pail, and hurried out the door.

She barely had time to relax against the pillows before he was back. Without having to be told, he went to her stash of rags, folded one carefully, and soaked it in the cool water. Then he picked up a cup and scooped up some of the liquid as he sank down on the mattress beside her.

"Should I mix some of that powder ye use in here?" he asked, offering it to her.

Smiling slightly, she took it from him, but had to use both hands to keep it steady. Blessed Virgin, she was tired. The last day had been emotionally exhausting, and the bairn was obviously making her weepy, because the knowledge that she was safe—and Rocque was sitting here caring for her—made her throat thick.

But she answered truthfully. "No' yet. I appreciate the offer, but methinks I should be awake for all of this."

Besides, she had something to ask him.

So, after sipping the water, she tightened her grip around the cup and watched him as he wrung the water out of the cloth and patted her burn.

God's Wounds! 'Twas agony!

But...but somehow, knowing *Rocque* was the one caring for her, she didn't mind the pain quite so much.

Who knew he had such gentleness in those big hands of his? Well, actually, she *did* know that; she'd been his lover for the last year. Tonight, she'd watched him snap a man's neck without even breathing hard, but he'd cared for her so gently, she knew he was capable of softness.

Soon, he'd hold their bairn that way.

Their bairn. Their cottage.

Aye. He was her man...and she was his woman. They'd be together.

Exhaling, Merewyn sunk further into the pillows.

"I am no' hurting ye, am I?" he asked with an anxious glance at her.

"Nay—aye, well, 'tis painful. But the cold water helps."

He looked so serious when he bent back over his task. "I could fill a barrel and dunk yer leg in it. Would that help?"

The image he presented had her smiling, remembering the way he'd dropped her in the stream to numb her pain. But he'd taken the time to keep her chemise dry, which showed his caring. Thinking of that now, she cradled the cup in one hand and used the other to self-consciously pull the rent in the garment closed.

It didn't really work.

The movement attracted his eyes, because he glanced up at her naked breasts. His gaze lingered there for a moment, but she didn't see lust in his expression—only sorrow. Finally, he met her eyes.

"I'm sorry I didnae get there sooner, lass. Ye'll never ken how sorry I am."

"Ye got there in time," she assured him. " 'Twas what matters. I wasnae sure what to do when he didnae go down."

The sorrow was still in his eyes, but his lips twitched under that beard of his, and he dropped his attention to her injury once more. "When I saw ye pick up that burning log, I almost yelled. I wanted his attention on me, but kenned he was still too close to you."

Dipping the cloth into the cold water again, he shook his head. "I couldnae believe ye *hit* him with it." When he pulled it out to squeeze the water from it, she could see his hands shaking the tiniest bit. "St. John's tits, Mere! I am sorry. I should've been there!"

Although his hands were gentle when he laid the cloth across her burn, she could see the coiled tension in his forearms, so she dropped her chemise and laid her hand there.

"Rocque, there's no need for forgiveness. Ye saved me." *Saved us.*

"If Jessie hadnae defied Hamish, and stayed to hear where ye were going..."

He wasn't looking at her, but Merewyn could see the way he'd clenched his jaw, and knew he was chastising himself.

"She came to find ye?" At his quick nod, Merewyn smiled softly. "Then she saved me just as much as ye did. God's Truth, Rocque, 'tis *my* fault for chasing ye away from our home."

At that, he finally looked up and met her gaze, his expression curiously blank.

Finally, he murmured, "Our home?" and sounded almost...hopeful.

She nodded carefully, suddenly nervous. She swallowed, then swallowed again. Why couldn't she say what she needed to say?

She'd waited too long, because his attention dropped back to her injury and he pulled the cloth from it one last time. He used the coverlet to dry the burn as carefully as possible, then reached for the jar of salve.

"I'm going to just dab this on, aright?"

He didn't wait for her agreement, but scooped up a tiny amount on his first two fingers, and reached for her burn.

Knowing she had to speak her question *now*, or she'd lose all courage, she blurted, "Ye said ye loved me."

He froze, his fingers hovering above her burn, for a few more heartbeats than was necessary. Then he exhaled.

And nodded.

His fingers dropped to the injury, and he began rubbing in the salve. She was so focused on him that she almost didn't feel the pain from his touch.

Finally, he said softly, "I do love ye," his attention on his actions.

"Why—why did ye no' say something?"

He still didn't look up. "Ever? Or last night?"

Last night—had it only been last night?—she'd been the one to tell *him* he didn't love her. And because he didn't love her, she wouldn't marry him.

God forgive her, she'd been so *certain*.

"Last night," she choked out.

"Because I didnae ken then." His movements still slow and deliberate—still not looking at her—he dipped his fingers into the jar again.

"And now?" she whispered.

He'd smeared the salve over almost all her burn before he blew out a breath and said, "And now I ken the truth." His blue gaze darted up once, then back to his work. "This feeling I have, 'tis love. I'm not certain I would have said something if ye hadnae confronted me last night." He finished coating the edges of the injury, but didn't look up. "And I might no' have had the ballocks to declare myself *now*, if ye hadnae just told me ye wear rosemary for me."

He loved her.

Merewyn's hands were shaking when she lifted the cup to her lips. He loved her.

But... "What does the rosemary have to do with...aught?" she asked, her lips hidden by the rim of the cup, trying to decide if the pounding of her heart meant she were about to cry or faint.

Taking a deep breath, he reached for the wet rag and wiped his fingers as he finally—*finally*—met her eyes. "Ye wear rosemary because ye ken I like it. Ye make my favorite meals...ye take care of me."

It wasn't a question, but she nodded. Of *course* she took care of him. 'Twas what she did.

"Ye care for me, Merewyn. No' just *taking* care of me, but ye care *for* me." Shaking his head, he dropped the cloth back into the bucket. "Och, I'm making a mess of this. My point is—I dinnae ken."

When he dropped his elbows to his knees and leaned forward to lace his fingers together, his broad shoulder turned her way, and somehow, that made it a little easier for Merewyn to breathe. She took another sip of water, and blinked away unexplained tears.

"Even if ye dinnae love me, Mere, ye care for me," he finally said in a low voice, staring at the colorful rug on the dirt floor. "Ye care for me, and 'tis enough for me to tell ye how *I* feel. Ye said ye wouldnae marry a man who doesnae love ye, so..." Taking a deep breath, he straightened, but didn't turn toward her. "So now I'm telling ye, ye willnae have to. I want to marry ye, and I—I love ye."

When he swung about, piercing her with a serious stare, she inhaled sharply at the intensity in those blue eyes.

"But, Mere," he said, reaching for the hand which wasn't holding the cup, "I also love ye enough to accept your decision if ye decide ye cannae marry a man ye dinnae love—"

"I love ye."

Mayhap she shouldnae have blurted it out so suddenly, judging from the way his eyes went round, but how could she *not*? How could she allow him to blather on, believing she didn't return his feelings?

With shaking hands, she placed the cup on the table beside the bed. "It took some time to admit it, aye," she whispered, "but my love for ye is why it hurt so much to think of spending the rest of my life with ye...ye no' returning my feelings." Swallowing, she met his eyes. "So nay. I mean, aye." She smiled softly. "Aye, I love ye, Rocque Oliphant."

His eyes darted between hers, as if looking for the truth. Finally, he nodded once, firmly, as if he'd known the truth all along.

But, "Good," was his only response to her confession. Then he squeezed her hand. "So I can ask ye again."

"To marry ye?"

He nodded.

I love ye enough to accept your decision...

Her heart pounding—knowing her answer already—she had to ask, "If I say nay, are ye really willing to accept my decision?"

Was that fear she saw in his eyes before he glanced away? "Aye." He swallowed.

Mayhap she wasn't doing either of them a favor, but she had to know. "And after ye accept my decision, ye'll go find yerself another woman to become yer wife, so ye still have a chance at becoming the next laird?"

He reared back as if she'd slapped him, dropping her hand. "Nay!" He shook his head, his mouth still twisted in a frown. "Mere, ye're the only woman for me. I thought ye understood that? If I cannae marry ye, I willnae marry."

He loved her.

He loved her enough to give up the lairdship.

Suddenly, he lunged for her hands again, scooping them both up in both of his. The movement jostled her leg, but the goatweed was beginning to work, and she barely felt the movement. Besides, she couldn't focus on aught but the intensity in his expression.

"Do ye no' understand, Merewyn? *I love ye.* That means I want ye, and only ye. Even if ye cannae have bairns, and I dinnae have a chance at winning my father's little contest—"

Cannae have bairns? "What?" she sputtered, her stomach flip-flopping.

Or mayhap that was his bairn, making his presence known.

"Well…" Awkwardly, he rolled his shoulders, but didn't drop her hands. "We've gone a year without a babe, aye? I ken ye've been…" He flushed, then swallowed, and jerked his chin toward the board with the marks hanging on the wall. "I ken ye count the days to prevent pregnancy." Was it her imagination, or did he sound a little *proud* he'd figured that out? "But…is that method always faultless?"

Unbidden, a little laugh burst from her, and she clamped her lips to contain another. Her heart was pounding, her stomach was clenching. She was nervous and excited all at once, anticipating what she had to tell him.

Or 'twas the ague.

One of the two.

Slowly, she shook her head. *Counting* was not always faultless…as evidenced by the fact she was pregnant now. Her *counting* had been flawed three fortnights ago.

He was staring at her as if he couldn't understand her response, but he nodded once, as if glad to have it all decided. "So I want ye to ken I dinnae care, Mere. Well, I *do* care, because I want bairns. But even if we must adopt children, I want to—"

"Let me get this straight," she interrupted. The laughter was threatening to spill out again, but it felt almost desperate now. Mayhap she was suffering some sort of infection. "Ye're willing to marry me even though ye think I might be barren?"

Meeting her eyes, he nodded solemnly.

He loves me.

This time the laughter *did* burst from her lips, but when it emerged, 'twas joyful. "Ask me again!" she demanded, using her grip on his hands to pull herself upright in the bed. "Now!"

He was frowning—likely thinking her mad by her reaction—but he clarified. "Ask ye to marry me?"

She was laughing too hard to answer, so she just nodded.

"Merewyn, will ye marry me? Be my wife?"

And just like that, her laughter turned to sobs, and she pulled her hands from his to throw her arms around his neck.

"Aye!" she cried against his chest. "Aye, I'll marry ye, Rocque!"

The sound he made was somewhere between relief and joy as he wrapped his arms around her and squeezed tight enough to push another sob from her.

"St. John's heart, love, I—God forgive me, I forgot about yer ordeal!"

He yanked her arms from around his neck, pushing her back, as if that would help. But she was laughing and crying all at once, and used the backs of her hands to wipe at her eyes.

"God's Truth, Rocque, the goatweed is working—I can barely feel my leg."

"But, yer tears…"

"Aye," she half-sobbed, half-laughed. "I am sensitive these days."

He was frowning when he stood and reached for her cup, then crossed to her little kitchen. *Their* little kitchen.

She settled against the pillows and tried to calm her breathing while she watched his nice-looking backside as he poured her some ale from the pitcher she kept on the counter for him.

Returning to her bedside, he thrust it at her.

"Drink this, lass. Ye're obviously having a delayed reaction to the shock."

"The shock of what?" she teased as she took the ale. "Agreeing to marry ye?"

"The shock of what happened— Och!" he burst out, when he realized she'd been joking, then planted his hands on his hips. "What is wrong with ye, Mere? Ye were crying a moment ago, and now ye're smiling. 'Tis like ye're..."

When he shrugged, she took a sip of the ale to calm her stomach and hide her grin.

"Mood changes are no' the only thing, lover," she managed in a serious tone, as she stared down at the cup. "I am more tired these days, have ye noticed?"

"Aye," he offered hesitantly.

She had to fight to keep her lips straight. "And places—like my breasts—are more sensitive to the touch. And I'm eating more."

"St. John's elbows, Mere!" Suddenly, he was on his knees beside the bed. "I *have* noticed!" He grabbed her hand, causing ale to slosh over her breasts and lap. "What is wrong with ye? Ye're the healer, ye should ken."

Carefully, she took another sip of the ale, then twisted to place it on the table, drawing out the moment.

"I *do* ken," she finally confessed.

He snatched up her other hand and pulled them to his lips. "Tell me," he commanded, placing a kiss on the back of each. "Ye've just agreed to become my wife, Merewyn, and I love ye. Tell me."

So, eyes twinkling, she did. "I am pregnant. With yer bairn."

He blinked.

Her smile finally bloomed. "I'm carrying yer bairn, and if the Oliphants are lucky, it'll be a son and ye'll be laird one day."

"Ye're pregnant?" he repeated.

She nodded.

"With my bairn?"

She nodded again.

"And ye hope 'tis a lad?"

Thinking this was getting repetitive, she nodded a third time.

Slowly, he lowered her hands, placing them gently on the mattress before him. Then he hoisted himself from his knees and stood. Moving deliberately, as if in a daze, he sat on the mattress beside her.

"I'm going to be a Da?" he whispered, staring straight ahead. "A father."

She shifted forward, resting her hand on his arm.

"Ye're going to be the best father, Rocque."

When he turned to her, there were tears in his eyes.

If she hadn't seen it—the big, burly Oliphant commander with *tears* in his eyes—she wouldn't have believed it.

"A da?" he whispered again.

This time it was *she* who pulled *him* into her arms, and he went easily, as if he was happy to be led around. With only a little wincing, she managed to shift over, pulling her chemise out of the way so he could lie beside her, his arms around her middle and his head pillowed on her breasts, which still peeked from under her torn chemise.

But he didn't seem to notice.

They laid like that for a long moment, his cheek pressed against her heart, until his arm moved, and he settled his big hand against her stomach.

Against his bairn.

"A babe," he murmured.

"Aye," she yawned. Her eyes were closed, her head tipped against the pillows. The laughter, the pain, the terror and excitement had drained her. Or mayhap the goatweed *was* affecting her. Either way, she felt boneless as his weight pushed her comfortably into the mattress.

"When?"

She understood what he was asking, and her fingers rose to play with the hair at his temples. "I'm only a few weeks along now. So mayhap a month or two after Hogmany?"

He was quiet for long enough she drifted in the darkness. But his words pulled her into wakefulness once more.

" 'Tis why ye have no' counted for the last moon, aye?"

"Aye. I'm sorry I didnae tell ye sooner. I didnae realize ye thought I was barren."

But he'd wanted to marry her, even if she was.

She felt his chuckle against her skin. "Ye should've heard Malcolm trying to explain yer cycle to me."

"Och, a woman's cycle is mysterious and wonderful—"

"And gross."

Smiling in the darkness, she sighed softly. He wasn't wrong.

After a long moment, she had to ask, "Ye're happy, aye?"

In a moment, he'd pulled her hand from his hair, and pressed his lips against her palm. "I cannae believe ye have to ask, love," he murmured against her skin. "I'm going to have a bairn, and ye're going to be my wife!"

The feel of his lips against her skin stirred a longing in her. She was too comfortable—and too worn out—at that moment to act on it, but she shifted slightly under him.

"As my husband, 'tis yer responsibility to drive away all memories of *his* hands on me."

He pushed himself up on his elbows, and she could see his grin, even in the dim light. "I'll do my best."

She yawned, then managed. "Now?"

Chuckling, he pushed himself upright, then to his feet, and padded across the room to blow out the candles. "Nay, no' now, love."

Darkness engulfed the cottage as she exhaled, drifting closer to sleep. She heard him remove his plaid, then the mattress shifted as he joined her. Although they both preferred to spread out as they slept, tonight, when he gathered her in his arms, she didn't mind it one bit.

"When?" she murmured, exhausted, but craving his touch.

His lips brushed against her hair. "Mayhap I'll wait until ye're my wife."

Darkness was closing in, but she smiled softly and burrowed into his hold. He'd keep her safe and warm and *happy*.

" 'Twould be cruel, Rocque," she whispered against his chest, "to make me wait so long."

"Then I'll wait for ye to heal."

"Even crueler."

He chuckled. "Go to sleep, Merewyn."

So she did.

CHAPTER 11

As the crowd of wedding revelers cheered, Rocque lowered his head to kiss his wife. *His wife*. St. John's knees, the thought made him proud!

Merewyn was finally *his*! Not just in the eyes of the clan, but in the eyes of God.

And she was carrying his bairn!

Grinning against his lips, she stretched up and wrapped her arms around his neck, twining her fingers through the hair at the back of his neck—hair she'd trimmed for him only that morning.

It had been over a sennight since the night she'd been taken by Hamish; the night Rocque thought he'd lose her. The night which changed his life forever.

Her burn had healed sufficiently, allowing her to walk and move without pain, although 'twould likely scar, she said. He didn't care; as far as he was concerned, she was still the most beautiful woman he'd ever seen.

And now she was *his*.

A slap on the back had him stumbling forward, but he wrapped Merewyn in his arms and protected her by pulling her to one side. Scowling, he twisted around and met his father's grinning gaze, his aunt on his arm.

"The two of ye are putting on quite the show, lad!" Da chuckled. "Mayhap ye should retire to yer cottage?"

The hoots of laughter and cheers from the crowd flustered Rocque, but Merewyn merely grinned and curtseyed.

"Laird Oliphant, how kind of ye to grace us with yer presence. And Lady Agatha." Another deep curtsey, and Rocque wondered if they would sense the sarcasm. "Ye're looking remarkably fit for a woman whose gout was so bad I had to get up from my sickbed, hobble my arse up to the castle, and massage ye two days ago."

"*First* of all," the old woman snapped, holding up a finger, "Whatever ye do to my foot, 'tis no' *massage*. Ye twist and pull until I'm ready to cry."

Merewyn grinned innocently. "That must be why ye always insist on me doing it, aye?"

Aunt Agatha scowled. "*Second* of all—well, I cannae remember my second point." As William Oliphant rolled his eyes, she held up a third finger. "And lastly, if ye really *were* in yer sickbed two days ago, ye should no' be dancing with this great oaf now, much *less* trying to taste his—his—what is that dangly thing in the back of his throat?" She turned to her nephew. "Willie! What is the dangly thing in the back of yer throat, which the Healer was obviously trying to lick?"

The laird reared back. "She was trying to lick *my* dangly thing?"

Aunt Agatha smacked his arm. "No' yer dangly thing, ye daft man. *Rocque's.*"

"Rocks dinnae have dangly things, Aunt Agatha," Malcolm drawled as he strolled up to the little group.

Rocque was pleased to see his twin, if only to have some backup in this strange group. Da was looking exasperated, but Merewyn was grinning as if she was enjoying herself.

He slapped his brother on the back. "Thank ye for yer help, Sir *Rocks Dinnae Have Dangly Things.*"

Malcolm blinked. "Is this a cock joke? 'Tis hard to tell sometimes."

Merewyn leaned in and lowered her voice. " 'Tis what she said."

As Da broke into loud guffaws and Agatha sniffed, Malcolm looked delighted. "I see ye've heard my latest invention, aye?"

" 'Tis yer joke." Merewyn snaked her arm through Rocque's arm, but nodded at Malcolm. "But I think the entire clan has heard it, thanks to Kiergan."

Agatha sighed. "That lad is helpless. Has the sense of humor of a— a—pickle!"

"A pickle?" Rocque repeated with a straight face. "Ye mean, something long and thick and bumpy?"

"And green and sour tasting, laddie," the old woman snapped, "So if ye're making another cock joke, 'twill take some stretching."

Da's eyes widened at his aunt's crude words, but when Merewyn nodded solemnly and whispered, " 'Tis what she said," he broke into guffaws again.

Rocque was busy chuckling himself, so when his father reached out and pulled Merewyn from his embrace, he didn't react quickly enough. Not that he would've stopped his father, really, but he *liked* having her in his arms.

But Da—big and brawny and bearded, an older version of Rocque himself—pulled her into his arms and gave her a hug strong enough to lift her feet from the ground. Rocque winced, wondering if that was safe for the bairn, but when Merewyn returned the hug, he quelled his urge to object.

After a long moment, Da set her back on the ground, and they were both grinning. "Welcome to the family, lass. I expect ye to give my lad many strong lads of his own, aye?"

Eyes twinkling, Merewyn exchanged a glance with Rocque. They'd decided—after discussions during the last week as she recovered—to keep the news of her pregnancy quiet for now. If naught else, they didn't want to alarm his brothers that they were ahead on the contest.

"Thank ye, milord. I am—"

But the older man just tsked and held her hand out for Rocque to take. "Ye're part of my family now, lass. Call me Da!"

Merewyn's grin bloomed, and this time her curtsey was more serious. "And can I call ye Aunt Agatha, milady?" she asked, clearly teasing.

But the old woman just waved her hand and rolled her eyes. "I dinnae see why no'—everyone *else* does."

Malcolm nodded seriously. " 'Tis true. Half the keep calls her 'Aunt'."

Nodding, Rocque pointed out, " 'Tis because she's related to half of them."

The old woman's hand lashed out, quick as lightening, and pinched Malcolm. "And I *want* to be related to *more* of them! When yer twin here presents yer father with a grandson—before ye, I'll point out, since ye're taking yer time!—he will be my great-great-nephew!"

Wincing, Malcolm rubbed his arm where she'd pinched him, and stepped out of her reach. "I'm no' *taking my time*. I'm going about the decision methodically and purposefully."

Da nodded. "The clan would do well to have a future laird who plans and thinks things through." Then he offered Rocque a smile. "Just as well as we'd do to have a laird who is strong and a good fighter."

Most of the clan had heard what had happened in the wood a sennight before; how Hamish had attacked Merewyn, how she'd been wounded, and how Rocque had killed the villain for his crimes. When Jessie had come forward with her story, they'd all been disgusted by the shite-weasel's plans, and agreed that a quick death had been too good for him.

Now, Rocque's gaze darted across the courtyard to where Jessie was dancing with Nessa as the two giggled together over something or other. 'Twas good to see the lassie fully recovered from her ordeal, and he felt a fierce sort of pride that he'd protected her as well as Merewyn.

Shifting his hold to her waist, he pulled his wife against his side, and when he met Da's proud gaze, he knew his father was thinking the same thing.

Suddenly, under the noise of the revelers and the music, Rocque heard a pounding. A sort of distant drumming, coming from the walls of the keep, which somehow still seemed to reverberate through the courtyard.

As Aunt Agatha cackled, and Da frowned thoughtfully, Merewyn turned in Rocque's embrace and smiled up at him. Distracted by the perfection she presented in his favorite purple dress, her red curls flowing around her shoulders, Rocque almost forgot to wonder about his father's expression. Da heard the drummer too? What did that mean?

"Bloody hell," Malcolm murmured beside him. "There goes that infernal drumming."

Well, *that* snapped Rocque's attention sideways. "Ye hear it too? Ye ken what that means?"

"*Dooooooooommmm!*" Agatha shrieked.

But Mal just rolled his eyes. "When I marry, 'twill no' be because hormones or *love* compels it, brother. Nae offense," he added belatedly to Merewyn.

"None taken," she offered with a giggle, twining her arms around Rocque's neck.

His twin continued. "When I find the right woman—and dinnae worry, Da, I'm compiling a list—*then* I'll propose marriage. We will go about this logically, instead of—of—"

"Hormonally?" Agatha offered.

"Exactly."

But Rocque wasn't paying attention anymore, because Merewyn was grinning up at him, and he could tell she thought Malcolm's theories were downright ridiculous as well. All she had to do was give him a little tug, and he went willingly, dropping his lips to hers.

It was the sexy little groan—too quiet for the others to hear—which she made against his lips that had him hardening under his kilt. Mayhap Da was right, and they *should* retire to their—*their*—cottage early.

"Och, there they go again!" he dimly heard Agatha snap in the background. "Malcolm, ye ken things!"

"All sorts of things, Aunt Agatha," Rocque's twin offered in a teasing tone. "I can tell ye how to calculate the circumference of a sphere, or about the cameleopard's grazing habits, or why the early martyrs most commonly—"

"What's the dangly thingy in the back of Rocque's throat? That the lassie looks like she's trying to lick?"

In his arms, Merewyn pulled away from the kiss, but not out of his embrace. Rocque was breathing hard, but 'twas hard to concentrate with the chatter around them.

"Well, I dinnae ken what *Rocque's* is called, Aunt Agatha. Stephen? Larry? Mongo?"

Agatha scoffed as Merewyn pressed her forehead against Rocque's neck. "*Larry?* Who would name their dangly thing *Larry?* Fergus now, Fergus is a fine name."

Malcolm's voice sounded strained when he replied. "Mayhap ye should suggest Rocque name his dangly thing Fergus."

As Merewyn began chuckling, muffling the sound against his skin, Rocque scowled over her head at his twin. "I'm no' naming my dangly thing *Fergus* or Larry or aught else."

"Uvula!" Da burst out, and when they all turned to him, he nodded happily. " 'Tis called a uvula."

"I cannae believe ye recall that," Malcolm said softly, obviously impressed.

But Da just grinned. "Yer auld father still has some brains left, lads. Now…" Taking his aunt's hand, he tucked it into the crook of his elbow again. "I can pick up on hints. I'll take Aunt Agatha over there to see Fergus, that fine warrior who arrived with yer sister-in-law Skye. He's been making eyes at my aunt all evening. I dinnae think I can take much more."

Agatha lifted her chin. " 'Tis what she said."

Silence met her joke. Da stared at her with an open mouth, Merewyn burrowed her face in Rocque's upper arm, and Malcolm made a sort of choking noise.

Rocque exchanged a glance with his father, and saw his own surprise reflected back.

Then, as if they'd both come to an unspoken agreement not to reply to the old woman's comment, they nodded and took a deep breath.

"Right." Da cleared his throat, then cleared it again for good measure. "Right. We'll...we'll go do that. Malcolm, ye run off and find one of yer other brothers to annoy or something to fix."

With an elaborate bow, Mal murmured, "I live to serve, father dearest." Then he winked at Rocque and strolled over to where Alistair was watching the festivities with a frown.

Da snorted, then jerked his chin toward Rocque. "And the two of *ye*, go back to yer cottage and get started on a grandson for me, aye? I dinnae want to have to tell the wee bairn how he was begat right here in the courtyard because his da couldn't keep his hands off his mam."

Merewyn smiled up at Rocque. "I believe our laird has commanded us to have sex, my love."

"Lots of it!" Da called over his shoulder as he led Aunt Agatha away.

And Rocque, ever the dutiful son, swept his wife up into his arms and, over her squeals of laughter, headed home.

THEY'D BARELY MADE it through the front door, before Rocque's hands were reaching for the ties of her gown. Laughing, Merewyn helped him, but as soon as the bodice loosened, his large hands snaked inside the material to cup her breasts, and her chuckles turned to moans of need.

"Blessed Virgin, I've missed this!" Arching her back, she pushed her mounds into his palms, even as she scrambled to loosen the rest of her gown.

As his callused thumbs brushed across her nipples, she felt a spark run from his touch down through her stomach to her aching core, and *tug*. Her gown dropped to her hips as she scrambled to yank her chemise down as well, and each movement—hers and Rocque's—sent her thighs rubbing against her wetness in a cruel mockery of what she needed.

"St. John's tits, Mere!" His voice sounded hoarse, and when she paused, already panting with need, he was staring at her almost reverently. "If I ever suggest we go this long without touching one another, slap me."

It had been *his* idea to sleep separately for the last sennight. He'd claimed it was so he wouldn't accidentally jostle her leg as she healed, but she wondered if he did it to heighten their eventual pleasure.

"Aye, husband," she drawled. But instead of slapping him, she reached for his belt and began to unravel his plaid, desperate for more of his body.

Instead of helping, he lowered his mouth to her breast, pulling one pebbled nipple into his mouth. Her hands froze as she forgot everything but her name and her next breath. Her entire *being* was focused on what his tongue was doing to her nipple, and when he hummed, she felt the reverberations through her whole body.

"Rocque," she whimpered. *"Please."*

He didn't speak, but transferred his mouth to her other breast, as he reached for his belt. In one swift movement, his kilt was on the floor, and he stood there in only his fine linen shirt. They must look a pair—him with his arse bared and her with her tits bared—but Merewyn couldn't care.

This was *Rocque*. Her husband.

He was hers, and she was his.

She knew his body, knew *him*.

And knew what he liked.

Desperate now, arching under his tongue, she reached blindly for the hem of his shirt, and fumbled beneath for his cock. 'Twas swollen and eager, and her mouth filled with saliva at the thought.

Nay, no' this time.

Neither would last long—it had been too long since they'd lain together.

He pulled away from her skin long enough to groan, "Ye're killing me, lass," and although she hadn't thought it possible, she felt him grow even fuller in her grasp.

"Turn around," he gasped, and she eagerly followed his command.

She only stumbled once on her way to the table, then she braced her arms against the wood and peered over her shoulder. Rocque had pulled his shirt over his head, and now stalked toward her, rubbing his own cock. Wide-eyed, she watched him pump at the shaft, spreading the bead of liquid from the tip all over its length.

Breathlessly, she lifted her eyes to his face, skimming across the broad chest, and saw the *need* in his eyes as well. She thrust her arse into the air, dropped her weight onto her elbows, and held her breath when he yanked up her gown to pile it atop her hips.

The cool air hit her wet, aching core, and she didn't bother hiding the moan which escaped her lips. And when he grabbed her arse cheek, dragging two fingers from front to back, her knees spasmed.

"Please, Rocque!"

And then he was there, his tip filling her. Together, they exhaled in relief as she sank back onto his cock, enveloping it fully. His strong hands locked around her hips—one atop her gown, the other beneath —and he moaned.

"Are ye ready, wife?" He sounded breathless.

Ready? God's Wounds, she'd been ready for *days*. Ready for *certes* since he'd kissed her there on the steps of Castle Oliphant. Ready to be his *wife*.

But instead of answering, she dropped her cheek to the wooden table-top, which thrust her arse further against him, and scrambled for the skirts of her gown.

As he began to thrust into her, she pulled aside the final piece of material, reaching for the pearl of her pleasure. She brushed a finger across it, and mewled in need at the sensation. God's Truth, when he took her this way, from behind, the way animals mated, she felt— there were no words for it, other than knowing *she'd* awakened this need in him.

She was powerful, and the way he was panting with each thrust told her so.

"Aye, give me yer seed, husband," she encouraged him, as he bent over her and planted one hand against the table by her head. "Make me yers."

"Merewyn," he groaned near her ear. "My wife."

When she stroked herself again, she shivered, thrusting back to meet his onslaught, and wrapped her free hand around his strong forearm. The Blessed Virgin knew she loved his forearms!

He rocked against her, his breath bursting from him with each thrust, and she stretched to reach back to her opening. Aye, she could keep the heel of her hand against the center of her pleasure, and use her two fingers to bracket his cock on either side of her core, prolonging his pleasure.

"Mere!" He reared up, away from her back, and his next two thrusts were strong enough to cause her to lose her grip. When he slammed into her like this—when all she could do was hold on to the table and remember to breathe as the pleasure tightened deep inside —her knees went weak and her toes curled.

He must've known, because between one thrust and the next, he flipped her over on the table.

One moment she was face down, the next she was staring wide-eyed up at him as he scrambled to move her gown out of the way. With one yank, he had it off her legs, throwing it to the floor beneath the table, and he'd pulled her stocking-clad legs up.

"Hold onto yer knees, wife," he growled, and then he was pressing into her again.

God save her, this position was even better! She felt his cock reaching *deep* within her, and she pulled her own knees back so he could sink in even farther as he held her hips.

Her mouth fell open, panting with desperation, and she *knew* the little mewls of pleasure coming from her lips were all that he wanted, and more.

He captured her gaze. "Now?"

"Please, husband," she moaned.

So he dropped his large hand to her pearl, and pinched it between his thumb and forefinger. Just the way she liked.

Screaming his name, she came apart, the white-hot pleasure exploding behind her eyelids as she thrust her legs out and around him, pulling—*pulling*—him closer. He roared wordlessly and pumped twice more, then froze as he spilled his seed against her womb.

God created sexual intercourse for the procreation of humanity.

Father Stephen's old sermon sprang into her mind, and Merewyn felt a giggle rising from within her. Procreation of humanity? She was already pregnant, but Rocque had spilled against her womb as if he intended to get her with child again.

Again? The giggle burst forth. 'Twas impossible to fall pregnant again while one babe nestled inside her. Her giggles turned to chuckles, and she felt his chest rumble with laughter as well.

"What are we laughing at, wife?" he finally managed to ask as he straightened away from her.

Reluctantly, she loosened her legs' grip on his hips, but reached up to pat his chest. "I dinnae ken!" but she continued to laugh.

And so did he.

They ended up on the bed, still chuckling, as he kicked off his boots and peeled down her stockings and slippers. Then he pulled down the coverlets and snuggled them both underneath, tugging her into his arms.

Neither spoke for a long moment, and she was afraid he'd fallen asleep. The wedding celebration had been boisterous, and she didn't begrudge him the ale he'd drunk when his men had offered toasts.

But eventually he stirred, and lifted his hand to stroke her hair. "I love ye, Merewyn Oliphant."

He'd sounded so reverent, she had to push herself up on her elbows to stare down at him. They'd left the candles burning, and she could see the serious look in his eyes.

"I love ye as well, husband. We're bound together, now."

"Aye, after I asked ye a half-dozen times."

She smiled, and dropped a kiss to his nose. "Ye ken my reasons. I'm sorry I didnae realize ye *did* love me. I'm sorry I was so fixated on ye saying the words, when yer actions spoke just as loudly."

He hummed and lifted one arm to rest behind his head, finally smiling. "And I'm sorry it took me so long to get my head out of my arse and figure out how to *tell* ye how I felt. I never should've made ye doubt my feelings."

"I suppose we're both stubborn fools, aye?" she asked, propping her head up on one palm while she rested her elbow beside him. Leisurely, she dragged her other hand down her breast, relishing the way her skin felt so *alive* after that climax.

His eyes followed her fingertips, and she knew the exact moment his interest turned from idle to aroused.

But still, he flicked his gaze back to hers. "What I want to know, lass, is *when* were ye planning on telling me about the bairn?" His large hand dropped from her head to her stomach, caressing the new life growing there. "Were ye *ever* going to tell me?"

"Och, dinnae fash," she assured him with a grin, rolling over to lounge across his chest. "I kenned I could never keep such a secret." She dropped a kiss to his nose again, then his lips, appreciating that he'd trimmed his beard for the celebration.

His hand slowly appeared from behind his head, and both settled on her hips. "So ye would've told me I had a bairn?"

She swung her leg over his, so she was straddling him. And when she felt his member twitch to life against the cleft of her arse, she grinned.

"Ye will be the finest father I've ever kenned, Rocque. I would never keep ye from yer son or daughter. I kenned that, even if I didnae swallow my pride and marry ye, ye would still be a part of our bairn's life." Slowly, she slid back, until her thighs bracketed his hips, and was rewarded by the way he swallowed suddenly. "Ye'd take care of both of us."

His cock now pressed against her, and the knowledge he was ready for her again sent a wave of desire pulsing through her. They'd both known, after their separation, that making love *once* wouldnae be enough.

Despite his clear arousal, Rocque's gaze was serious when he met hers. He cleared his throat. "I will *always* take care of ye. Ye, and any bairns God grants us. Even when I thought ye couldnae have bairns, I wanted ye to be my wife, Mere. I love ye."

He loved her enough to give up his chance at lairdship.

"I have to warn ye, lover. Just because I'm pregnant doesnae mean one of yer other brothers will no' beat ye in having a son. Pregnancy and childbirth are mysterious and unpredictable."

His lips twitched. "And gross."

"Aye, and gross."

Now there was a light of teasing in his gaze as he dragged his hands up her hips to her sides, spanning her waist with his hands. "I ken I can lead the Oliphant warriors, Mere, and I ken I'd be a good leader. But I'm no' as good with people as Finn is, or as smart as Malcolm is, or even as dedicated as Alistair." His palms skimmed her skin as they rose to tease the outside of her breasts. "If I'm no' the next laird, 'tis because God had other plans for me and my brothers."

He was the best man she knew. "And ye're aright with that?"

Smiling, he cupped her breasts, and she shuddered.

"Love, I have a cozy home to return to each evening, good food, a supportive family, and a wife who loves me. What more could I ask for?"

Each of his thumbs brushed over her now-pert nipples, and she moaned.

"The question is, *wife*, if *ye're* aright no' being the next Lady Oliphant."

She never wanted to be a lady. She was a healer, and soon she'd be a mother. She had a fine husband, and was certain of her place in the clan.

Things were perfect the way they were.

Her smile turned to chuckles as she leaned forward, pushing her wet core against the base of his shaft, even as she pressed her lips to his neck.

"Let me show ye just how *aright* I am."

Chuckling, he wrapped her in his arms and pulled her lips to his.

Aye, this was where she belonged.

In her husband's arms.

EPILOGUE

HANDS CLASPED BEHIND HIS BACK, Malcolm strolled to where his brother Alistair was standing, sipping an ale and frowning at the festivities.

"Och, dinnae say ye're thinking of work ye can be doing?" he admonished teasingly. When Alistair startled, Malcolm continued, " 'Tis a celebration! Sometimes work can be put aside."

His brother didn't reply, but took another sip of his drink.

Malcolm settled beside him, and together they watched Finn and Duncan spin their wives—their identical wives—around in time to the music from the pipers and fiddle. Other married couples were smiling breathlessly at one another as they danced, and the unmarried lasses were being handed from one beau to the next as each tried to claim their hands.

But none of them were the one Malcolm wanted.

"Do ye ever think," he suddenly asked, "that they're going about it all wrong?"

"Wrong?" his brother repeated. "In what way?"

Shrugging, Malcolm tried to put his thoughts into words. "This... falling in love. 'Tis no' *logical*. Marriage is an arrangement, naught more. For certes, I'd like to be attracted to my wife, if I am to get sons on her. But…" He waved his hands at their married brothers. "Why bring *love* into it?"

Beside him, Alistair snorted softly. "Love is well and good, if ye have time for it. But ye're right; a marriage is an arrangement, and I dinnae even have to be attracted to a wife to marry her. I'd need to ken she's from a strong clan so our alliances will be useful. I need to ken she brings a dowry which will strengthen our own clan—land or goods or whatnot. And *then* I need her to leave me alone."

With raised brows, Malcolm glanced at his brother. In his mind, marriage had always been a partnership; a business arrangement. But what Alistair was saying…

"Ye want her to focus on her duties so ye can focus on yers?"

Alistair shrugged. "And why no'? If I cannae take time away from my duties to *find* a wife, I dinnae expect to have time to devote to her when I am actually *married* to the woman."

Ahh. "Ye're still hoping to talk Kiergan into wooing one for ye?"

His brother's scowl returned, only this time 'twas directed at Alistair's twin across the courtyard, who was laughing at something Lara had just said. " 'Tis no' a *hope*. He'll do it for me, *eventually.*"

The two men watched the merriment silently for another few minutes, until Malcolm's thoughts couldn't stay silent. He shifted, then exhaled in exasperation.

"I dinnae mind devoting time to my search—I've *been* devoting time to it. But I willnae allow my *heart* to make a decision for me, when I have a perfectly useful brain to do it."

Alistair hummed. "Ye're still looking for a widow?"

"A widow with *sons*," Malcolm corrected. "Young enough to bear more for me, and her sons young enough to ensure her womb is still prepared to carry a son."

"Is that…how it works?"

Malcolm opened his mouth to deliver a lecture to his brother, but could tell Alistair wasn't interested. So he just shrugged.

"More or less," he muttered, unwilling to admit that while the hypothesis was strong, he hadn't done the research to test the theory.

Alistair downed the rest of his ale. When he lowered the flagon, he belched and slapped Malcolm on the back.

"Well, brother, I have that list of crofters ye asked about. I'm no' sure ye'll find yer widow here on Oliphant lands, but if she's here, we'll find her."

"Thank ye." Malcolm allowed himself a small smile. "I also have Aunt Agatha on the case, when she's no' yelling about *doom* and that damned drummer."

"Excellent! She seems to ken everyone who has ever even crossed through Oliphant land. And aye, 'twill do her good to have a distraction from her obsessions."

Obsessions? Oh, Alistair had meant the drummer. "If only the damned fool would learn to drum during the *day*! But I suppose he wouldnae be a Ghostly Drummer if he didnae practice at night."

"Ye've heard him, then?" Alistair's brows went up.

"Och, aye," Malcolm spat, glaring up at the stone walls where he'd so recently heard the infernal pounding. "Have ye no'?"

For the first time Malcolm could recall, his brother appeared…flustered.

"Ghosts dinnae exist, Mal," he muttered, staring down into his empty flagon.

Malcolm noticed he hadn't answered the question.

But then Alistair shook his head and his smile looked a bit forced when he nodded. "I cannae take the time to look for my own bride, so I'm damn well no' helping ye find *yers*. But if ye join me in Da's solar tomorrow, I'll get that list for ye."

"My thanks." Malcolm settled back on his heels to watch the revelers. "I am no' picky. As long as she meets my requirements, she'll do."

And he meant it. Find him a young enough widow with a son, and he'd marry her. Any woman would do.

AUTHOR'S NOTE

AUTHOR'S NOTE
On historical accuracy

This is the third book of the *Hots for Scots* series, and hopefully you've read the first two well enough not to expect any *actual* historical accuracy in this one?

Good. There's very little history in here, after all.

Instead of worrying about things like geography, timeline or, you know, *history*, in this book, I tried to cram as many cock jokes as possible.

'Tis what she said.

HA! Okay, that's the last one, promise.

But yes, this series is all about humor instead of setting or history. The only thing I'm going to point out is that yes, Merewyn's herbal medicine is all accurate. Goatsweed, or St. John's wort (and snail slime, *eew*!) was used by medieval herbalists to treat burns. Autumn crocus, musk mallow, and all the other herbs I mentioned were used in those contexts. Even hemlock was used as a painkiller and sedative...but too much can be deadly, because it literally works by slowing down your body's functions.

Also, before I get readers up in arms about Merewyn's ability to live alone as a respected member of the clan, let me just say: *Excuse me*, strong and independent women have been a part of our history for millennia. Healers like Merewyn would've been vital to the continuing health of the clan, and would've been considered powerful members of society.

Shacking up with the clan's military commander wouldn't hurt, either.

I've been excited to write Rocque's story since he first popped, fully formed, in my head. My husband named him, and it was such a hilariously cheesy name, I knew from that moment exactly who Rocque would become. But you know who I'm *really* excited to share with you? Rocque's twin brother, Malcolm.

Malcolm has overcome the same difficult past as his brother, but it's clearly affected him differently. He's the intellectual, the scholar of their group, and he's completely certain he knows *exactly* how to find a wife.

Surely he'll be successful, right? Skip ahead to read a sneak peek from *In Scot Water*.

But first, I want to offer you a personal invitation to my reader group. If you're on Facebook, I hope you'll consider joining. It's where I post all the best book news first, and you'll be able to get to know me personally. My Cohort is also instrumental in helping me name characters and choose covers! So stop on by!

Okay, who's ready for a little peek at Malcolm's story? Here's the prologue from *In Scot Water:*

"Is that her?"

At Malcolm Oliphant's side, his brother looked down at a ledger he carried, back up at the woman across the square, checked the ledger once more, and grunted.

"Aye, she matches the descriptions I received. Evelinde Oliphant and her two sons come to market on the third Thursday of the month." Alistair scowled up at the dark storm clouds. "No matter the weather."

Despite the impending weather, Malcolm only had eyes for the lass arguing with the cloth merchant. "She's beautiful," he breathed.

She *was*. Her long black hair was pulled back in a simple braid, and she moved with a grace he hadn't often seen. But as she turned away from the merchant—part of the haggling, judging from the way the portly man began to wave his arms to call her back—Malcolm sucked in a breath at the quiet serenity in her face.

That, and the signs of her exhaustion.

What must it be like, to be a woman living alone with her two young ones, far from any civilization? Alistair's records showed Evelinde had been born a MacRob, and her Oliphant husband had built a croft close to those lands so she could visit her kin. But that meant she was several hours' travel from the village or any other towns.

His brother Alistair cleared his throat.

"I'll admit yer scheme to find a widow with sons was a smart one, brother. But I've taken time from my work to help ye, and now ye've spied one ye obviously find pleasing."

Malcolm slapped his brother on the shoulder, distractedly. "Aye, and ye have my thanks."

"We're about to be hit with a deluge." Alistair sounded exasperated. "So go over there and *speak* to her."

Speak to her?

Speak to that angel? The angel who looked harried as she carefully counted out money with one hand, while holding onto the hand of what looked like a rambunctious lad with the other? He was yanking at her arm, trying to direct her attention to the baker's shop, and she was speaking quietly to him *and* the merchant.

There was a baby strapped to her chest with a piece of Oliphant plaid. Another son, according to Alistair's records and the research Malcolm had done.

Aye, she was exactly what he was looking for.

So why couldn't he march across the square and swoop her up? Why couldn't he speak to her?

He knew how the Earth rotated. He knew how mushrooms reproduced. He knew the major arteries of the human body, and the bloodlines of the great kings, and how to employ levers and fulcrums to simplify structural modifications.

But he didn't know *this*.

"Well, Mal?" His brother sounded exasperated. "Are ye going to speak to her?"

She turned away from the cloth merchant, a bolt of simple green wool in her arms, and met Malcolm's eyes.

And he couldn't move.

She was beautiful, aye, but delicate. Gentle looking. *Exhausted.*

The lad was tugging her, and with a soft smile, she allowed him to lead her toward the delicious smells wafting from the baker.

She had enough on her mind and enough to handle at this moment. Malcolm had the certain sense that, were he to go to her right now, he would only add to her burdens.

"Mal?"

"Nay," he choked. "The time is no' right."

But as he watched her glance over her shoulder at him once more, Malcolm knew the truth; she *would* be his.

***

Evelinde couldn't help risking another glance over her shoulder. The two men who'd been staring at her were still there, and the one on the right...

Well, she'd never believed in the kinds of connections Father Ambrose had always spoken to her about. She certainly hadn't felt that tug with her husband. Nay, she'd married him for the security he could offer her—after years spent relying on the charity of the church, she'd been happy for a home of her own—not because of how he made her feel.

But *that* man...

When she'd turned away from the wool merchant, having parted with more of her precious funds than she'd intended, she'd met his blue-gray eyes, and had felt the tug, the pull, deep in her soul.

And something had stirred in her stomach, something which was connected to the place of her desire, and she instinctively pressed her thighs together to capture the sensation.

There was *promise* in the man's gaze, and she could feel it.

Even from across the square.

"Mama! Mama, I want a honey bun."

She turned her attention back to her son, where it belonged. "Aright, my wee honey bun."

Four-year-old Liam giggled. *"And* a wheat loaf?"

Her monthly market visit meant treats the lad looked forward to as much as she did. "Aye. I'll get two, *if* ye're willing to carry the basket home."

"Aye! Aye!" the lad was bouncing up and down. "Ye carry the baby, I'll carry the food."

Smiling tiredly, she let him lead her to the baker. They had a three-hour walk home, and she knew she'd end up carrying both her sons *and* the basket by the time they reached halfway. Her back ached to think of it.

Sometimes she wished she could leave Liam home with Nanny, as she did when she went foraging. But on market days she was gone all day, which was too long to leave him. Besides, the lad was curious and full of energy, and craved the sights and sounds of civilization as much as she did.

"Come along, my love," she called softly to him as the reached the shop.

Before speaking with the baker, she turned once more to the spot where the men had stood earlier, hoping to catch one more glimpse of the tall, auburn-haired warrior who'd made her breath catch.

But he was gone.

———————

Ready to find out if Malcolm un-chickens-out and chases down Evelinde? Check out *In Scot Water!*

ABOUT THE AUTHOR

Rocque Oliphant has simple wants: a fine sword at his hip, a good meal in his belly, and a lusty wench by his side. His position as the Oliphant Commander, leader of men, ensures the first, and his long-term affair with Merewyn, the clan healer, ensures the second and third. She brings him joy—and pleasure—in ways he once only dreamed of!

Aye, things are going well in his life...at least they were, right up until his father—the laird—demanded he marry and start producing grandsons. If Rocque wants to beat his brothers at a chance for the lairdship, he needs to find a willing woman to bear his sons—and fast!

But Merewyn, the stubborn lass, refuses to marry him and won't tell him why. Rocque can't imagine spending his life with anyone else! So if he can't marry another lass, and the one he wants won't marry him, what chance does he have to secure the title of the new laird?

As the Oliphant healer, Merewyn knows her value to the clan. She is also quite aware she doesn't *need* to marry...and the only way she will, is for love. And Rocque, stubborn idiot that he is, won't tell her his true feelings. Can she be blamed for saying *nay* to his proposal? But now she's running out of time and knows she has no choice but to tell him the truth, or set him free, because in a few months, everyone in the clan will know her secret!

Rocque might have more brawn than brains, but he's smart enough to know he can't lose Merewyn. But is he prepared for the battle it's going to take to prove that to her?

Warning: This story contains naughty bits. Lots of them. *Ridiculous* amounts. Also contains characters and conversations which are funny enough to make you spit out your tea. For the sake of your Kindle, do not drink while reading this book. That is all; you may now carry on.

Manufactured by Amazon.ca
Bolton, ON

15224325R00090